JOKER'S PLAY

Joker's Play

All rights reserved
Copyright 2011 Major Mitchell and Jerry Mitchell

This is a work of fiction.
All characters and events portrayed in this book are fictional,
and any resemblance to real people is purely coincidental.

Reproduction in any manner, in whole or in part, in English
or any other language, or otherwise without the written
permission of publisher is prohibited.

For information contact: Shalako Press
P.O. Box 371, Oakdale, CA 95361-0371
http://www.shalakopress.com

ISBN: 978-0-9830608-2-6

Cover Photograph by Major Mitchell
Cover design: Karen Borrelli
Editor: Judith Mitchell

Dedication

To the lawmen who tamed the west.

JOKER'S PLAY

By Major Mitchell and Jerry Mitchell

Shalako Press
Oakdale, CA

JOKER'S PLAY
A Clay Best Novel

The morning sun had begun to peek over the top of the scraggly trees lining the hill east of Cool Water. Clay Best approached the dismal cemetery north of town. The slight breeze failed to disturb the dusty haze that clung to the sky, giving the air a bitter alkaline taste. Texas was well into a second year of drought, with little promise of it ending soon. If the old Indian at the Rio Grande crossing was right, the hot, dry weather would continue for several more years.

Clay dismounted and loosely wrapped the reins to a rickety fence post, then hung his black jacket over the pommel. He patted the black mustang on the rump and picked his way through the scattered graves. He was a tall man, lean and powerfully built, with dark brown eyes to match his moustache and hair, which were now beginning to show flecks of grey around the temples. His choice of black attire and black horse made his presence even more imposing, which suited him well as a lawman. He was also a man who seldom smiled. He went about his business quietly, never asking much from others, and expecting little.

The small bouquet of wildflowers he was carrying was sad-looking, and wouldn't last but a few hours in the heat. He made his way toward a fresh grave where he stopped and removed his hat. He laid the flowers carefully on the tiny mound before kneeling in the dirt. The sun cast its early morning light on the crude wooden marker, making the carving legible: *June Elaine Best, 1844 – 1885, Into the hands of God.*

He broke into sobs as one of the petals fell from a yellow sunflower and fluttered away in the breeze.

"I'm sorry, June. They were the best I could find. This heat's about burnt up everything. Oh, God, I should've been here. You should never have had to go through dying alone."

He took his time composing himself as he blew his nose on a crumpled handkerchief and shoved it back into his pocket.

"Well, I finally done it. I quit working for that tight-fisted bastard. I know you never liked hearing me cuss, but ol' Lester Bishop's lucky I didn't blow his brains out, after ordering me to chase down a couple of two-bit rustlers, knowing you was that sick. I should never have brought you to this part of hell. You were an honest-to-God lady, and deserved more'n the likes of me. You should've been married to someone who treated you right. I never knew why you loved me like you did."

Clay traced his fingers across the crudely carved angel at the top of the marker.

"Raul did a nice job on your marker, considering what he had to work with. I hate to leave you like this, but if I don't shed Cool Water, I'll wind up shooting Lester to hell, and I know you'd hate that worse. So, I'm heading to Carrizo Springs. Maybe I'll find a hunk of land and start a spread of my own…get out of the law business altogether. I'll come back and visit as often as I can, as soon as I get over hating Les so much. He jerked his head upward and reached for his gun as a shadow passed over him, but relaxed as his horse stopped at the edge of the grave as though he had come to pay his respects.

"She was a lady, Loco. Too good for the likes of us."

Clay dusted his pant-legs and led the mustang out of the cemetery before tying his jacket to his bedroll. He climbed into the saddle and paused to stare toward June Best's grave before nudging Loco forward.

"We'll be back, June. I promise."

Chapter 2

Teresa Romero woke early. She made a pot of strong coffee and slipped into a white cotton dress with blue and red bands around each sleeve and the bottom hemline. She buckled a braided belt snugly around her waist and pulled on sandals, then tied her long raven hair back with a bow before taking a sip from her favorite mug. She spent a quiet minute savoring the flavor, watching the chickens scratch and peck around in the yard. She set the empty mug aside and attacked her daily cleaning chores before the day's heat made it almost unbearable. She had discovered long ago that living in a *jacale* at the edge of Carrizo Springs required daily dusting and sweeping, or the Texas desert would soon reclaim her home.

Teresa had inherited the place from her grandparents after her grandmother's death six months earlier. Her grandfather had built the *jacale*, using pickets of mesquite and elm taken from the creeks, lashing them together with smaller branches and rawhide. He had then plastered the inside with a mixture of clay and gravel. The hut was crude, but had served her grandparents well. Juan and Yolanda Perez had taken Teresa in after both of her parents had been killed during a Comanche raid on their farm. She had only been a toddler at the time, and had trouble remembering her real mother and father. Teresa had begun to consider the aging couple as her parents early in life. Her grandfather's death had hit her hard. Then she met Refugio.

He was the most dashing man that fifteen-year-old Teresa had ever seen. She had been helping her grandmother make fresh tortillas over the grill in the front yard when a group of riders passed. She quickly recognized them as the banditos from across the border that everyone had been talking about. One of them stopped near their picket fence and removed his sombrero before flashing a brilliant smile.

"*Buenos dias, señorita.* I am Refugio Romero. We have just ridden from Mexico and are planning to spend a few days at Carrizo Springs. I could not help but notice your beauty. I wish to beg your parent's permission to come visit your casa, if I may."

That was all it took for her to decide that Refugio would become her future. At first her grandmother, Yolanda, did not like Refugio in the least. But she finally relented and allowed them to get married following Teresa's sixteenth birthday. Refugio proved to be a good husband and lover when he was around, which was seldom. Being a leading member of a gang of bandits and a revolutionary required him to be away for months on end. Teresa spent her lonely hours at the church, praying for his safe return. She shook her head as she dusted the well-worn curtains. It was ironic that he was killed in the dusty street in front of their casa. She had forgotten to pray for his safety at home.

Teresa would turn twenty-six next month and realized for the first time, as she poured another mug of coffee, that she was totally alone. Yolanda had been her last living relative. She had hoped to have children of her own by now, and maybe even own a small café. She was a terrific cook. Her food was much better than the slop the owner of the cantina served. But none of her dreams had become a reality.

But they will, Teresa assured herself as she vigorously swept the hard-packed dirt floor. *My prayers to Saint Joseph will be answered. He will send someone into my life to give it meaning.*

She leaned the broom against the back wall and washed her face and arms, then scattered the remaining water across the floor in an effort to keep the dust down. She would refill the bucket later from the spring, but the sun was beginning to turn the outside into an oven. It was past time to do her daily shopping. She grabbed the knitted bag she used to carry her goods, and shoved a straw sombrero tightly on her head. Walking briskly toward the center of town, she raised small clouds of dust with her sandaled feet.

Life had taught Teresa several harsh lessons. She never kept vegetables or meats that could not be eaten in one day inside her *jacale*, because they would spoil in the relentless heat caused by the drought. Another lesson involved trusting men. In her loneliness, she had invited the owner of the cantina into her house for supper one night, and received thanks by getting beaten and raped. The horrible man then bragged of his accomplishments, making it sound as though she had been the aggressor. A steady line of men began hounding her as a result. She finally had put a stop to the nonsense by shooting at several of them with Refugio's pistol. The last lesson was never to keep money inside the *jacale*. Her grandmother and husband had left her precious little, and the last time she had kept any at home, it had mysteriously disappeared. She suspected the cantina owner of this also, but had no way of proving it.

Her first stop would be at the bank to draw out just enough pesos to get some fresh vegetables and meat for that evening's meal. She noticed a man sitting on horseback as she approached the bank, but thought nothing of it. She paused when she noticed the man was holding the reins to two other horses, when there happened to be a hitching rail not three feet from where he sat.

She glanced around and spied another man across the street dressed in black, standing near a black horse. He was a tall hombre, who seemed to be taking his time packing tobacco into a pipe. He struck a match against a post in front of the general store and lit the pipe before glancing her way, then led his horse between two buildings and out of sight.

Shrugging, and thinking it all meant nothing, Teresa entered the bank and froze as a man pointed a large pistol in her face.

"Geeze, woman!" He grabbed her and flung her across the room before kicking the door shut. "Don't just stand there like a jackass!"

"Got it all," a second said as he came from behind the counter with several bags. "Let's git!"

"Hold it," the first man said. "We're taking her with us."

"Why? She'll slow us down."

"'Cause some big guy was watching the bank a few minutes ago from across the street. He ain't there now, but I got me a feeling. I'd rather have a hostage and move a little slower, than move faster and end up dead."

"Well, grab her and let's go."

Teresa caught her breath as the man grabbed her wrist and jerked her toward the door. She pulled back with a cry of pain but quit resisting as he pointed the gun at her face.

"You're going...one way or the other. You get to choose."

Teresa Romero walked obediently in front of the man toward the waiting horses. Her life suddenly had meaning, but not like she had hoped.

Chapter 3

Clay knocked the ashes from his pipe after only three puffs, and shoved it inside his saddlebag. It had been three months since he had left Cool Water. He had stayed mostly to himself during that time, wandering from town to town and camping in the desert as he waited for the searing pain inside his chest to ease. He was a man that normally took charge and saw that things were done properly. He figured that people should live according to the laws of society and plain decency. June's death had hit him hard. Kneeling beside her grave, he had suddenly realized there were some things he had absolutely no control over. There were no trails he could ride, no guns he could shoot or battles he could fight that would bring her back. He could not pass any ordinance that would cause her to walk through the door smiling. The empty hole inside his chest where she used to live could not be filled.

But he knew that June would never want him to waste away feeling remorseful and bitter. She had been full of life, even in her sickness, so it was high time he started living like a human again. He had discovered an abandoned ranch a few miles outside of town in his wanderings, and had decided to see if it would be possible to buy. He didn't have much, but perhaps he might be able to swing a line of credit at the Bank Of Carrizo Springs. He had checked into the hotel, bathed and put on a fresh change of clothing. He was rehearsing a speech inside his head as he walked Loco toward the bank, but stopped across the street and dismounted when he saw the rider in front of the bank.

Clay stood in the shade of the general store, packing his pipe as he studied the situation. Someone waiting in front of a bank might mean nothing under normal circumstances, but it was too hot to be sitting on horseback in the sun. Besides, no self-respecting cowhand would be holding the reins of two extra horses when a perfectly good hitching rail stood empty only three feet away. Mostly though, it was a simple gut feeling that caused him to lead Loco between the buildings and check the loads in his gun. He was already in the saddle and moving toward the edge of town when he heard someone shouting that the bank had been robbed. Supposing the bandits would be heading toward the border, Clay was surprised to see an extending cloud of dust leading northwest away from town. He turned Loco and urged him into a ground-eating lope in the direction of the dust.

The bandits stayed with the road for several miles before detouring into the brush almost due west. Clay slowed Loco to a trot as he followed, careful to save his mount from exhaustion or a crippling chuckhole. The bandits on the other hand, seemed willing to punish their mounts, forcing them through thick brush and clumps of cactus in an effort to hide their trail. Clay shook his head. They were either foolish, or had more than likely stolen their horses and planned to abandon them the minute they found others to steal.

The ground grew hard and rocky in places, making the trail difficult to follow. Loco was beginning to suffer from the heat, and Clay figured the men would have to stop soon, or be on foot. He slowed Loco to a walk as the trail turned south. Then it veered back west a quarter of a mile later, directly into a clump of salt brush and mesquite.

Clay sat for several minutes, waiting to see if the men would continue through the brush, but they never appeared. A thin line of green snaked its way from the rocky hills to the north, and passed through the clump of mesquite before continuing south. He turned Loco, trusting the thick brush to shield him from view, and dismounted a hundred yards south of the mesquite. Following the line of green brush, he found a small trickle of water. He loosened Loco's saddle and allowed him to drink a little before leading him to a shady spot to cool down. Then he washed his face in the stream and felt the sting of alkali against his eyes. After a few minutes he allowed Loco to drink a little more water and took a swallow from his canteen. Clay pulled his rifle from the scabbard and injected a shell into the chamber. It was time to get down to business.

He could hear them talking as he crept through the brush.

"I tell you I seen someone out there."

"Well, where'n the hell are they? You've been sayin' it for the past half-hour."

"Aw hell, Orville, give it up. Me and Joe's gonna count the money."

Clay crept closer, inch by inch, until he thought he was close enough, then eased a branch on a greasewood bush back for a better view. They had the woman lashed to the gnarled trunk of a mesquite bush while they hunkered in a circle surrounding a saddle blanket piled high with the stolen money.

"Whoeee," one of the men shouted. "There's $1,400.00, if I calculate right."

"Yeah, and it's all ours," another laughed.

"We'd better be gitting. They'll be sending a posse after us soon," the third said. Clay eased the branch back and ducked as the man glanced around.

"Hell, Orville, a bloodhound couldn't foller us the way we come."

"I wouldn't be too sure about that myself. Besides, Orville's right. The horses are rested. We'd best be heading out."

Clay slipped to his right behind a pile of dry tumbleweeds as they talked.

"What about the woman?"

"Hell, you brung her, Orville. You figure out what to do with her."

"Leave her. She's slowing us down."

"Leave her way out here alone?"

"Got any better suggestions? Wanna take her back to town?"

"No, but…"

"Well, you can argue all you want, but I'm gonna see what she's really like before we leave her. Hold her down, Orville."

Clay wormed his way into position as one of the men untied the woman. He eased the Winchester into position, but pulled back as the woman attacked the two men like an angry badger.

"Aw, Gawd! Grab hold of her, Walt," Orville yelled as she clawed at his face.

Walt grabbed her by the hair and flung her to the ground. Orville immediately pounced on her, pinning her arms to the ground as Walt undid his britches, and let them fall around his ankles. He was in the process of trying to hike up the woman's skirt when she kicked him square in the face. He toppled over backward with a howl of pain as his two partners laughed.

"Stupid bitch broke my nose!"

"Hell, leave her and let's go," Joe yelled as he stuffed the money into the canvas bags.

"Not 'till I even the score." Walt swiped the blood from his crushed nose and grabbed a forty-five from the gunbelt lying on the ground. He aimed it at the woman and Clay pulled the trigger on his Winchester. The bullet took him square between the shoulder blades and knocked him into the mesquite. Orville jumped to his feet clawing at the pistol in his belt. Clay's second shot hit him in the chest. Clay turned to get a quick bead on Joe, but the man had disappeared through the brush.

He cursed under his breath and scanned the thick brush for any sign of him, but found none. Easing toward his right,

Clay circled the small clearing, stopping every few feet and listening for any tell-tale sound or movement in the brush. Nothing. The air seemed to be void of movement and hung thick, as sweat trickled from under his hat to sting his eyes.

He eased past a greasewood bush near Teresa and found himself staring down the barrel of a .44.

Chapter 4

Clay's knees almost buckled as a gun thundered. The bandit's head gave a quick jerk to the left as he fell to the ground. Clay stood frozen as the Mexican girl ran forward yelling curses in Spanish. She pointed the smoking gun at the man before spitting in his face.

"I reckon he's dead, ma'am." Clay caught his breath as she jerked the gun up toward his face.

"Whoa, whoa there!" He raised his hands. "I'm on your side."

"Who are you?" She kept the gun pointed in his direction. She was beautiful, but in a wild sort of way. Her thick black hair was a tangled mess, speckled with chunks of mesquite and dried grass. Her angry eyes were dark pools as they flashed across him, taking him in from head to foot in seconds. They had torn her dress, and it hung loosely, revealing one shapely breast. Clay cleared his throat before speaking.

"Name's Clay Best, ma'am. And I'm the one that killed them other two."

"You were in front of the bank. I saw you. Are you one of them?"

"No, ma'am. I had my money in that bank, and I wanted to get it back."

"*Si*, they stole mine also." She lowered the gun slowly and pulled the torn dress over her breast before spinning around and spitting out more curses at the dead men. Clay's

Spanish was limited, but he understood enough to know the lady was wishing the men an extended stay in the hottest part of hell.

"Yes, ma'am. I reckon that's where they'll be," Clay said as he collected the guns. "I also reckon we'd best toss their carcasses on their horses and be heading back. We've got a long, hot ride ahead of us." He began to tighten the cinches on one of the horses, but paused to stare at her.

"By the way, ma'am, I never caught your name."

"I am Teresa Romero. And I thank you, *señor*, for coming to my rescue."

"The feeling's mutual, ma'am." He gave the cinch a jerk and went to the second horse. "I thought I was a goner. You certainly saved me for sure." He paused to stare at her once more as she struggled to make the torn dress stay up. She caught him staring and turned away.

"I reckon you'd like something to cover yourself with, especially before we ride into town. If you want, you can follow the creek that-a-way until you find my horse. His name's Loco. He looks mean, but he ain't. I got an extra shirt in one of the saddlebags. You can slip it on and bring Loco back here."

"*Si, gracias, Señor* Best."

Clay watched her until she was out of sight, then shook his head and chuckled as he finished with the saddles. She was one hell of a woman, he'd give her that. While she'd saved his bacon, he didn't know whether he'd actually saved her. She would have been plenty for those three to handle. He draped the heaviest man over one horse, and the other two over another, saving the third horse for Miss Romero. He was in the process of tying the men to the saddles when she returned, leading Loco. She was wearing his white shirt with the shirttail tied snugly around her waist and the .44 tucked inside the braided belt.

"I saved one of the horses for you to ride. Those numbskulls abused these critters, and they're plum tuckered out. We'll have to take it slow heading back to town."

"*Gracias, Señor* Best. You are a kind man."

"Well, I don't know so much about that." He gave the rope a final tug and turned to discover she was already mounted on the spare horse.

"Well, I was gonna offer you a hand and help you up on that critter, but I see you don't need any help."

"I've ridden before, *señor, gracias.*"

"Yes, I reckon you have." He checked the cinches on Loco and patted the horse on the rump.

"You had enough rest, you ornery cuss. It's time you started earning your keep." He climbed into the saddle and took the reins to one of the horses, then began picking his way through the brush and cactus, back toward Carrizo Springs. He glanced back to see Miss Romero leading the other horse closely behind. She had straddled the horse like a man. Her skirt had hiked up, revealing a pair of shapely calves. Her sombrero had been lost somewhere during the chase, and she was wearing one of the bandit's hats with the leather drawstring tucked under her chin. *Yes, sir*, he thought. Teresa Romero made a striking figure. But he'd seen her other side. The man draped over the horse she was leading would testify to that fact…if he could talk.

Chapter 5

The sun beat down mercilessly, burning his back through the heavy cotton shirt. Sweat streaked his dusty cheeks and dripped onto the saddle as Loco picked his way slowly through the brush. The horse's black coat was plastered with white lather by the time the road to Carrizo Springs came into view. Clay looked back to see Teresa following thirty yards behind. Her horse was close to collapsing. He guided Loco toward a clump of brush near the road and dismounted. His nickel-plated pocket watch said it was nearing four o'clock.

"Better dismount and rest these horses," he said, as she reined up beside him. "If we're lucky, we just might make it to town before dark."

"That's good," she said, and slid to the ground. "I will be happy to say goodbye to our friend." She removed the hat and wiped her brow against the back of her hand. "He is starting to smell."

"Yeah, I reckon we're all starting to smell just a little. I'm gonna soak an hour or two in the tub when I get back to the hotel."

Clay gave her his canteen before digging the pipe and tobacco from his saddlebag. She took a couple of tiny swallows and passed the canteen to Clay as he sat beside her in the scant shade of the bush. He took a drink before packing the pipe.

Teresa sighed deeply. "*Si,* a good long bath sounds good, *Señor* Best. I will do the same. I will wash your shirt." She glanced downward and plucked at the front of the sweat-soaked cloth. "You may have it back tomorrow, if you wish."

"Tomorrow, or the day after will be fine." He struck a match and drew deeply on the pipe. "Reckon I'm not going anywhere soon."

"You are new in town. What brings you to Carrizo Springs, *Señor* Best?"

"Call me Clay." He took a puff and stared into the distance, seeing nothing. "I lost my wife, June, a little over three months ago. We were living in Cool Water, about ten miles or so south of here. Ain't much of a town. Ain't much of anything, to tell the truth. Anyway, old Lester Bishop owns the town and everything around it. He hired me as town marshal. A lawman's all I've ever been. To make a long story short, all I ever did at Cool Water was chase down rustlers and Indians. I was out on one of them chases and came back to find June had been dead and buried almost two weeks. No one had bothered to send word." He wiped his sweaty face with a grimy hand.

"I was hoping to make enough money to take June to Arizona, or somewhere where the air's cleaner. She'd been sick for some time. I never got the chance, and I knew I had to leave Cool Water, or I'd wind up killing Les Bishop. The old skinflint son-of-a-bitch." He took a puff to discover the pipe had gone out.

"Pardon my language, ma'am. What about you? What's your story?"

"Much the same, *Señor* Best. The Comanche killed my mother and father when I was a child, so my grandparents raised me. But they were old, and now they are both dead. I was married once." She lifted her head and smiled.

"Yes, ma'am. I figured a pretty young woman like you might be. Where is your husband?"

"The Comanche killed Refugio in the street in front of my *jacale*."

"I'm real sorry to hear that, ma'am." Clay struck another match to re-light the pipe.

"*Si*, Refugio was a revolutionary and rode with Bernal. He was a good man and a good husband, but he was away for long periods of time fighting the revolution. I would go to the church every morning and every night and pray, asking the Holy Mother to keep my Refugio safe and bring him home to me. But I forgot to ask her to keep him safe at home." She shook her head. "Now we are both alone, *señor*."

"You knew Heraclio Bernal?"

"*Si*, he ate at my table and I rode with them once, but my Refugio did not like it. He was afraid I would get hurt."

Clay nodded silently as he drew deeply on the pipe. He'd heard enough about Heraclio Bernal to fill a book. The man called himself a revolutionary, and claimed to be interested in the welfare of the peasant citizens of Mexico, but in reality he was nothing but a thief and killer. He led an army of pistoleros that numbered close to a 100 men, who robbed stagecoaches, attacked armories, raided mines and robbed rich citizens on both sides of the border. It was evident Teresa believed her husband and his boss were noble and honest men, but in Clay's book they weren't much better than the three men draped over the backs of the horses they were leading.

The sound of beating hooves against the sun-baked road drew their attention toward the north, where a cloud of dust was fast approaching.

"Well, I reckon we're not alone after all, ma'am. Looks like we've got ourselves plenty of company." Clay knocked the ashes from his pipe and returned it to the saddlebag.

Teresa made an attempt to swat the dust from her torn dress and adjusted the bandit's hat snuggly on her head as the posse drew to a halt in front of them.

"Well, well, what do we have here?" Sheriff Ray King said as he dismounted. "I might've known you'd run 'em down one way or the other, Clay. I wish you would've waited around another ten minutes and let us tag along. It would've saved us a long dusty ride for nothing."

"Ten minutes would have been too long, Ray. They were fixing to put Miss Romero on a stage to eternity when I come up on them."

"You were supposed to be tracking for us, Roy. What happened?" The sheriff glared at a heavyset man who scampered around, looking at the ground for tracks. "You're the one claiming you know how to track, but you led us right by this place, and took us several miles north."

"I do, Ray. But this is rocky ground. I must've had dust in my eyes." He scowled as several members of the posse laughed.

"Hey, Ray, take a look at this," one of the deputies yelled. He was holding one of the dead men by the hair and staring at his face. "It looks like Joe Donaldson and the Leech brothers finally got what's coming to them."

The sheriff studied each face carefully for a few seconds and grinned. "Well, it couldn't have happened to a nicer bunch. Now, let's get 'em into town. They're already starting to stink up the place. I'll need you two to stop by my office and give your statements."

"Yeah, I reckon I know the routine, Ray. Hope you've got something to drink besides water."

~ ~   ~

Sheriff King stepped out of the office while Clay scribbled his statement and Teresa dictated hers. He returned a few minutes later with a glass of red wine and a bottle of bourbon. He gave the wine to Teresa, then asked Clay to pour the bourbon as he removed his hat and gunbelt. He leaned back in his chair with a sigh and sipped the bourbon while he read their statements.

"Very neat," he nodded, "a few misspelled words, but neat." He pulled several wanted posters from a drawer and passed them to Clay.

"You might be interested in taking a look at those. Those boys had money on their heads. $150.00 on each of the Leech brothers, and $250.00 on Donaldson. I reckon you've got $550.00 coming."

"No, sir." Clay snickered as he shook his head. "I've got $300.00 coming. It was Miss Romero who did for Donaldson."

"That right, Teresa?" Ray asked. She calmly sipped the wine and stared at the wanted poster in her lap.

"Yeah, she did," Clay said. "I got the other two, but Donaldson slipped into a clump of bushes, and I couldn't see him. I went looking, and walked right smack into the muzzle of his gun. I figured I'd just bought the farm when Miss Romero put a hole through his head."

All three jerked around as someone pounded loudly against the door.

"Well, well, Henry," the sheriff said as he opened the door. He glanced at his pocket watch as the red-faced banker rushed into the room. "It took you all of ten minutes to show. I figured you would've been here five minutes ago. What took you so long?"

"I was busy, Ray. Is it true? You recovered all the money?"

"I didn't, these two citizens did," he said, gesturing toward Clay and Teresa. That son-in-law of yours couldn't track a buffalo inside a parlor. He led us on a wild-goose hunt. These folks had things all tidied up and met us on the road back into town. You ought to be thanking them."

"Oh, I do, I do," the banker said, giving both of their hands a vigorous shake. "You've saved me from disaster. Now," he paused and glanced around the tiny office, "I'll just collect the money and start an audit."

"Well, don't let us hold you back." The sheriff reached under his desk and produced the bags with the money. "I'll need an exact accounting of how much is in those bags."

"I thank you both again," Henry said as he opened the door.

"I'll just follow you over to the bank and take care of some business, if you don't mind," Clay said as he got to his feet.

"Oh, I'm sorry, but the bank's closed until I can complete my audit. I have to make sure everything is in order, you understand."

"All the money's there, if that's what you're worried bout. Miss Romero and me's seen to that."

"I'm sure you are correct, Mister...ah," the banker hesitated.

"Best, Clay Best."

"I really am thankful for your service, Mr. Best. But I do need to complete an audit, so I'm closing the bank until further notice." He rushed out, closing the door with a bang.

"Well, I reckon that's that." Clay frowned as he nodded thoughtfuly.

"Yeah, I've known Henry Jenkins for several years now, and he's a stickler for rules. You couldn't budge him with a stick of dynamite." Ray laughed. "I'll have Leonard Harralson over at the paper take a picture of the Leech brothers and Donaldson. I can submit the forms in the morning. It might take a week or two before the reward money arrives. I'd offer you both some walking-around money in advance, but I'm afraid everything I've got is in the bank. That's the best I can do."

"I reckon that's fine, Ray." Clay shook the sheriff's hand. "I've got a few dollars to get by. I was hoping to talk to that fellow about taking out a loan to buy that spread a few miles west of town. I was told the folks that owned it up and moved back east."

"The old Johnson place? Yeah," Ray nodded thoughtfully, "yes, they did. Too bad they cashed in. I reckon the combination of drought and the Comanches raiding their cattle kind of did them in. I understand the bank owns the place now. You ought to give 'ol Henry a day or two to calm hisself down and go talk to him."

"I reckon I might do that. I'll be over at the hotel if you need me." He shook the sheriff's hand one last time and held the door open for Teresa.

Chapter 6

"You are staying in the hotel? *Carumba!*" Teresa shook her head and laughed.

"Why, what's wrong with it?" Clay asked as they crossed the street.

"People who stay at the hotel lose things."

"Oh." Clay nodded. They walked in silence toward the edge of the town where Clay had left Loco at a crude thatched stable and corral which was made of crooked mesquite branches. Teresa addressed the owner in Spanish. The horse and its owner would be well taken care of.

"Come," she said with a grin as she took Clay's arm. "I will show you where I live. You may wish to rescue your clothes from the hotel, if they are still there, and stay at my *casa*. It is small, but it is much cleaner and your things will be safe. I cook better food than you will find in the cantina."

"I appreciate the offer, ma'am, and I'll take you up on the meal, but folks might start talking if I bunked at your place."

"They will talk anyway, *señor*. You cannot stop them from talking. They are like chickens making noise." She held her right hand up and moved it like a puppet, mimicking a mouth. "They talk and say bad things after the pig who owns the cantina said we were lovers, but it is not true. And I will shoot him if he ever comes near my *jacale* again."

They stopped in front of a crude hut with chickens pecking in the yard.

"This is my *casa, señor*. You are welcome here."

"Well, I'll tell you what I'll do, ma'am. I'll go clean up and be back here in an hour to eat supper. How's that sound?"

"*Bueno*," she said with a nod, but quickly covered her mouth and giggled. "*Perdon, señor*, I forget. I cannot fix you something to eat tonight. I have nothing to prepare. I was going to get some pesos from the bank and go to the market when those men took me. I will cook for you *mañana. ¿Es que está bien*?"

"That would be fine, ma'am, but if you ain't got no fixins around here, what are you gonna eat?"

"Oh, that is no problem. I will be okay. I will take a hot bath and find something to eat."

"Well, I'll tell you what, ma'am," Clay dug some gold coins out of his pocket, "you go fetch us some vittles while I get cleaned up. I'll be back in a couple of hours."

"But *señor*, this is too much." She tried giving him back part of the money, but Clay refused and turned away.

"You got that wrong, ma'am. It ain't near enough. You saved my life back there. Remember?"

Teresa watched the tall, soft-spoken man walk toward the hotel, before dashing into the house. She tossed the money on the bed and quickly fetched a bucket of water from the spring behind her house. She drank a dipper full and scrubbed some of the dirt from her face, then donned Refugio's sombrero and almost skipped to the market.

Teresa had stayed mostly to herself after the incident with the cantina owner, and had few friends. Almost eight months earlier, a young man named Rob Mayfield had come to Carrizo Springs and stayed at her casa for a few days. While they were not lovers, he was a good friend, and she liked him. He had a bother named Billy, but Teresa did not like him at all. She had sensed something evil in the man, and it was he who had talked Rob into going with him to Cool Water, where he said a man owed him a large amount of money. Neither of them had ever returned, and she knew something bad had happened.

Clay Best reminded her of Rob. He was much older and taller, but he had kind eyes and was a gentleman around her. She also knew the tall man could be dangerous when necessary, because she had seen him kill two men earlier that day. But he had treated her with respect, the same as Rob Mayfield had done. She carefully chose a melon and several onions, then argued with the owner about the freshness of a slab of pork.

Rob was supposed to return to Carrizo Springs and help Teresa open her own restaurant. She had taught him how to make tortillas and *salsa caliente* in the short time they were together. He was a hard worker and eager to learn. She doubted that Clay Best would ever make *tortillas* or *mole' con pollo*, but she felt safe around him, and she had not felt safe since Rob left.

She carefully chose her chilies, then a good bottle of wine. With this much money, she could prepare an entire fiesta for *Señor* Clay Best. It would be a meal he would not forget.

Chapter 7

Clay stared at the wardrobe and dresser containing his personal items. He didn't have much, but the few things he owned had been rifled through, with little effort to conceal the intrusion. He heaved a sigh and emptied the drawer into a carpetbag. Perhaps the woman was right. She had lived in Carrizo Springs nearly all her life, and knew the ins and outs of the community, including who not to trust. He didn't like the idea of becoming a burden in someone's home, especially to a widow. But that seemed preferable to having his things picked through by a thief when he was out and about.

He tossed the key on the counter as he passed through the lobby. "You're leaving us, Mr. Best?" the clerk behind the counter asked. Clay went through the door without answering. He walked briskly toward the stable, and thought briefly of asking Miguel if he could rent a stall to sleep in, but stopped in front of Teresa's *jacale* instead. It would only be for a few days at the most, until he could talk the bank into lending him the money to buy the Johnson place.

The chickens clucked and scattered as he closed the gate. A fire had been built in the outdoor pit, and the smell of spicy pork drifted to his nostrils. His stomach growled as he rapped his knuckles against the doorpost.

"Yes?" Her voice drifted from somewhere in the back.

"Miss Romero?"

"Yes, I am out back, *Señor* Best."

He shooed several chickens away as he walked toward the rear of the house, and almost ran into her as he rounded the corner. She was standing in the doorway to a small, three-walled lean-to combing her long black hair.

"*Perdóneme, por favor*, but I have tangled something…" she said as she struggled with a particular spot on the back of her head.

"Here, let me have a look-see." Clay dropped the carpetbag and took the comb. He took his time, carefully working the tangle out of her thick hair.

"You have done this before, *Señor* Best."

"Yes. I've done it a time or two. I used to brush June's hair for her, especially near the end. She got tuckered out and needed help doing most things. I didn't mind much. She waited on me most of the time we were married."

"You loved her very much, no?"

"Yes, I reckon I did. Still do, for that matter."

"I am sorry, *señor*. I shall remember to say prayers for her."

"Thanks, I'm sure she would appreciate it. There, I think I got the bugger out." He handed her the comb. "Whatever you're cooking smells wonderful."

"*Gracias.* I make *el chili verde con puerco.* I will start the tortillas now." She eyed him from head to foot, before staring at the carpet bag.

"You have had some trouble, *señor*, no?"

"Just a tad. Someone went through my things while I was gone. They didn't get much, except a few trinkets. I always keep my extra guns and valuables in my saddlebags, where I can keep an eye on 'em. Anyway, I figured if that offer still stands, I'd just as soon pay you to bunk here, than give my money to a bunch of thieves at the hotel."

"*Si*, I have an extra bed. I will make it for you after we eat. But you said you wanted to bathe. I will heat you some water first. There is a small mirror on the wall where Refugio would shave."

"Thanks." Clay picked up the bag and stared at the brass tub inside the lean-to. "I'm surprised no one's taken your tub, the way they steal things around here."

"Antonio watches," she motioned toward the sleeping dog. "No one bothers when I am away." The large mongrel yawned and stretched as she patted his glossy fur.

"He's a fine looking critter, alright. But if you don't mind me saying so, he doesn't look like much of a threat."

"That is because you are with me, *señor*. Do not come inside the gate when I am not here. Call at the gate and I will come, or Antonio will hurt you."

"Thanks, I'll remember that." The dog stretched once more, and gave Clay's leg a sniff before following his mistress inside. The mere size of the animal would cause most folks to consider staying outside the gate, whether she was home or not.

Clay placed his bag on a crude bench inside the lean-to and dug out his razor. He had finished shaving by the time she returned with a pail of steaming water and dumped it in the tub. He climbed into the tub and began scrubbing at the grime before realizing he was bathing in the same tub and water Teresa Romero had bathed in. He paused and stared at the bar of lye soap in his hand, then shrugged. Being raised the third in a line of six children, he had washed in the same tub his three younger brothers had scrubbed in. It would have taken too long to heat a fresh tub for everyone in the family, and water was scarce in parts of Texas, especially now. He figured another year without rain, and they might all turn to dust and blow away.

~   ~   ~

She had the table piled with tortillas, pork smothered in green sauce, and a bowl of steaming rice.

"You may sit there, *Señor* Best." She motioned toward a chair as she rummaged through a crudely-made cabinet.

"It smells wonderful," Clay said as he took the chair. The dog crossed the room at a lazy walk and snuggled against his leg. "The way my stomach's growling, you'd think I ain't ate in a week of Sundays."

"We shall cure your stomach tonight." She set two small porcelain cups that were decorated with bright Mexican flowers on the table, and uncorked the wine. "It is ready, *señor*, please…help yourself." She filled both cups with wine and passed one to Clay.

"Don't mind if I do. Here's to you, ma'am." Clay toasted her with his cup.

"No, here's to *us*, *señor*. If you had not followed those men today, we would not be here."

"Okay, to us."

~   ~   ~

Clay sat on the couch as Teresa cleaned the dishes. The combination of wine, hot food and the heat of the day was causing his eyelids to droop. He had no idea when he had dozed off, but woke early the following morning, lying on the sofa and covered with a thin blanket. He could hear Teresa singing as she prepared breakfast over the outdoor kitchen. He needed desperately to visit the outhouse, but Antonio was staring intently at him, with his muzzle only inches from Clay's face. The dog's breath smelled like stale corn tortillas. Clay decided to wait until Teresa came back inside. He only hoped it would not be too long.

Chapter 8

"I'm sorry Mr. Best, but the land you're speaking of doesn't belong to this bank. I wish it did. It's a valuable piece; it's worth more than what they're asking. The Bank of San Antonio holds the mortgage, not us. We're just a small local bank."

The pudgy banker's thinning hair was plastered against his glistening scalp as beads of sweat trickled down his puffy cheeks. It was only 10:30 a.m. and the heat was already climbing. It promised to be another scorcher.

"I understand all that, Mr. Jenkins." The crease between Clay's eyebrows deepened. "But I'd rather deal with you, right here in Carrizo Springs. I want you to lend me the money. That way, I just come in here every month and make my payment, instead of having to mail it all the way to San Antonio. It's safer and faster that way."

"Yes, and I agree with your logic. I wish I could accommodate you, but this bank has seen some tough times the past two years, with the drought and people leaving. We simply don't have that kind of money. If I lent you the money to buy the Johnson place, we wouldn't have any operating capital. When the folks who live here need to make a modest withdrawal, or take out a small loan, I couldn't help them. I doubt that the bank in San Antonio would sell us the loan on credit, seeing as we are strapped for cash. We simply don't have that much leverage. That's why the board of directors would only allow me to give you and Mrs. Romero a twenty-five dollar reward each for recovering our money. I honestly wanted to give you much more, and argued. But they simply wouldn't allow it."

"So, you're saying the two hundred dollars I've already got in your bank, plus the three hundred I've got coming for killing them thieves, and the money I got for recovering the bank's money still ain't enough to make a down payment to get a loan from you?"

"That's about the size of it, Mr. Best. I wish you luck in San Antonio."

~ ~ ~

Clay's luck didn't improve with the bank manager in San Antonio.

"I'm sorry, Mr. Best, but I'm afraid I can't help you. That property consists of 20,000 acres of prime Texas ranch land, and already has the improvements."

"I've been there. That's why I want it. It's also one of the few places around here that's still got plenty of water. All I have to do is start building a herd." Clay shifted in the chair, trying to find a more comfortable position.

"Yes, I'm sure you're right in your assessment. But even at today's prices, that land is still worth $29.00 an acre. Where does a man like you expect to come up with $580,000.00, Mr. Best?"

"I'm gonna make a down payment with the $500 I've got, and you're gonna lend me the rest. Then, I'll pay you back when I start raising cattle."

"Well," the banker raised his eyebrows and chuckled, "I must say I like your sand, Mr. Best. Yeah, I really like it. You're a true Texan, through and through. In another time and market, when we weren't facing a drought with a down economy, I'd be willing to take that gamble. I believe a man like you would certainly make it work. But I'm afraid the board of directors would take me out and hang me, if I loaned you the money."

He stood and shook Clay's hand.

"I wish you all the luck in the world, Mr. Best. I honestly do.'

~   ~   ~

He returned to Carrizo Springs late in the afternoon, four days after leaving, discouraged and tired. He left Loco with Miguel and walked slowly toward Teresa's *jacale*. He paused under the shade of a locust tree for a minute, taking in the view. She was in the front yard, singing as she stirred something in a cast iron skillet on the outdoor stove. The dog rose from his shady spot on the porch and trotted toward the fence. He gave three friendly barks, and she looked his way.

"Oh, *Señor* Best." She slid the skillet off the grill and opened the gate. "You are back. Did you have a good journey?"

"No, I actually had a lousy one. Howdy, Antonio," he said, giving the dog a pat.

"No? Oh, I am so sorry. Here, let me take those," Teresa said, grabbing Clay's saddle bags. "Come inside and tell me about it."

Clay sat on the edge of the sofa and pulled off his boots.

"Ah, Lord, that feels good. There ain't much to tell. I told them I wanted to buy the Johnson place, and they told me no. I didn't have enough money, no cattle, and nothing but a dream."

"But dreams are what make us great people," Teresa said as she uncorked a bottle of wine. She filled two cups and sat beside him. "Here, this will make you feel better."

"Thanks. I feel like I could use something stronger," he said with a chuckle, and took a sip.

"*Si?* I shall give you tequila with supper. But you are hot and dusty from your ride. Sit here and enjoy your wine and I shall heat some water for your bath. I must check on your *nopales*."

"I don't know what they are, but they smell mighty good." Clay took another sip of wine and leaned back to close his eyes.

"*Nopales* are made with eggs mixed with *carne* and cactus. We shall also have rice and *frijoles*. You rest while I get water." She hurried toward the door, where she stopped and looked back.

"Oh, I forget. Two men come here from the village of Cool Water looking for you."

"Well, I reckon it was a good thing I was gone. I might've shot 'em. Did they say who they were and what they wanted?"

"*Si*. One says his name is Dusty, and the other says he is called Utah. Are they bad men? I offer to cook for them."

"Naw, Dusty and Utah are okay. Wonder what they wanted. Did they say?"

"No, but they say they will be back tonight. Oh," she glanced toward the grill, "I must go."

"Well, whatever it is, it can wait until my brain cools down." He downed the last of his wine and closed his eyes. Teresa had to wake him to tell him the bath was ready.

Chapter 9

"Lordy," Dusty said over a mouthful of *nopales*. "I can see why Clay's been bunking here, ma'am. This cookin's the best I've run across anywhere."

"*Gracias*. Please, have another tortilla." She passed a wicker basket lined with towels and filled with steaming corn tortillas.

"Whoa!" Utah breathed heavily. "That sauce is hotter'n burnt gunpowder." He took a gulp of tequila mixed with lime.

"Why'd you boys come looking for me?" Clay asked before popping a forkful of beans into his mouth.

"Ol' Lester Bishop's lookin' for you. He sent us out to find you and bring you back," Dusty said with a grin.

"That ain't likely. You'd have one hell of a time dragging me back to that hole, and I'd kill that old bastard if you did." Clay gave him a toast with his cup of tequila. "You can go tell him that for me."

"I reckon I'd love to see his face when he hears it, but the thing is…me and Dusty ain't going back," Utah said with a snicker.

"You ain't?"

"Na, we've had enough," Dusty said. "Besides, there ain't nothing left of Cool Water. The cattle's either dying because of the drought, or being rustled right under Lester's nose, and he can't see it. There's only a few head left, and all he does is sit in his saloon and drink."

"Stolen's more like it," Utah said. "Dusty and me think it's them two slingers he hired just before you left. Both of 'em are more crooked than a dog's hind leg."

"Yeah, with you gone, there's no one to stop 'em from doing what they damned well want. Pardon me, ma'am," Dusty said with a glance at Teresa.

"Well, I could care less what happens to the old skinflint. I'd say he's getting exactly what he deserves."

"Yeah, but it ain't about the cattle," Utah said. "It's about Ruth."

"Ruth Bishop? What'd she do? Give a second look at some puncher working for her grandpa?"

"No," Dusty said. "She's been kidnapped. Someone ran off with her and left this here note." He reached inside his vest and handed Clay a sweat-stained piece of paper. Clay took his time unfolding the letter and reading it. The handwriting was crude, and smudged.

I have your granddaughter, Ruth. I want $25,000 in paper, placed in bags and left inside the old adobe church outside Carrizo Springs no later than noon Tuesday, or you'll never see her again. You are to leave the money inside the chapel and go. If I see anyone, anywhere in sight, she dies. If I pick up the money and anyone follows, she dies. My partners will kill her if I do not show up with the money by midnight. Remember, if anything goes wrong, Ruth dies.

"Well, I reckon that seems plain enough," Clay said, passing the note to Teresa. "When did he get the note?"

"This morning. We heard you were in Carrizo Springs, and the man at the stable told us where to look." Dusty said.

"Today is Friday," Teresa said, passing the letter back to Clay. "Is he going to pay them for his granddaughter?"

"No, ma'am. Mr. Bishop don't part with money too easy. Utah and me are taking bets as to whether or not he'll let her become coyote bait before he parts with that kind of money. All he said was, he wants Clay to find the men that took her, and bring them and Ruth back.”

“Ol’ Les sent every rider he has out looking for her the instant his housekeeper found the note on Ruth’s pillow, but she’s vanished. No one’s seen hide nor hair of her,” Utah said. “That’s why he sent us looking for you. He figures you’re his best bet for getting her back.”

“Huh, he more’n likely wants to keep his money, and put on a show about caring what happens to his granddaughter.” Clay snorted.

“*Señor*, we are talking about a little girl, and someone has taken her. Don’t you feel some…how do you say,” Teresa motioned with her hand, trying to grab the word out of thin air.

“Compassion,” Dusty said.

“*Si*, compassion,” she said with a nod.

“Shore I do. Outside of June, Ruth Bishop was the best thing around that hole. I never understood how someone as sweet and kind as Ruth could be kin to someone like Les. But I still ain’t that interested in working for the man.”

“*Señor*,” she laid a hand on his wrist and gave a gentle squeeze, “she is a little girl who needs you. Please…”

“First off, she ain’t so little. She’s what…nineteen by now?”

Utah gave a nod.

“Second, I’ve got no way of knowing where they took her, and I ain’t got enough money to go traipsing all over Texas looking for one woman.”

“Mr. Bishop said to tell you he’d pay you a thousand dollars to bring her back,” Dusty said.

“He did? Why don’t you boys find her and keep the money?”

‘We thought about it, but he said he wants you. Me and Utah’s heading to California.

“*Señor* Best, it will help you buy your ranch,” Teresa said with pleading in her eyes.

"I reckon it might, if he actually paid me when I brought her back. But there's one little thing no one's mentioned. I was involved in something like this once before. They took a banker's wife and left a note demanding ten thousand dollars. He paid it, just like the note said. I found her body a week later. Whoever kidnapped her slit her throat the minute he got the money. Dead folks don't talk too good. I'll guarantee you," he thumped his fingers against the table, "if we go looking, we'll find that Ruth Bishop's already dead."

Chapter 10

"*Señor* Clay. *Señor* Clay, wake up. It is time to go."

"Huh? Oh…!" The pounding inside his skull felt like a stampeding herd. The voice was Teresa's, but when he opened his eyes everything looked blurry.

"*Señor* Clay?" The blurry figure moved away with a giggle. "I think our *Señor* Clay Best had too much tequila last night, Antonio. Why don't you wake him?"

"Aw, Gawd!" Clay tried pushing the dog away as it swiped a large tongue across his face, but Antonio was persistent.

"Alright, alright! I'm awake."

"Antonio. Good boy," she said, patting the animal's furry side. Clay opened one eye in time to see her give the beast several stale tortillas.

"How is your head?" she asked with a grin.

I don't know, I ain't found it yet. Whatever this is on my shoulders feels like it's about to bust."

"You did not have to finish the last of the tequila after your friends left. That is what you get with too much tequila, *señor*." She stood over him grinning.

"You look terrible. Wash you face and I shall bring you coffee."

~   ~   ~

Finally, after two flour tortillas filled with scrambled eggs and peppers, and drinking three cups of black coffee, the pain inside his head had slowed to a dull ache. He stood in the shade of the front porch sipping a fourth cup and staring at the three horses tied in the shade of the locust tree.

"Maybe my eyes still ain't working, but that black horse looks strangely like Loco."

"*Si*, that is your horse." She looked up from the soapy pan as she washed dishes. "The *caballo rojo* is mine. His name is Diablo. I had Miguel saddle them, and also ready a pack horse for our journey."

Clay squinted at the large red horse next to Loco. They were almost the same size. "Journey? Are we going somewhere?"

"*Si*, don't you remember? We are going to find that poor man's granddaughter, and he is going to give us one thousand American dollars." She grabbed a white towel to dry the dishes.

"Huh." He tossed the remnants of his cup into the yard, and several chickens scattered. "I remember some things, but they ain't the same way you're remembering them. I recall something about Ruth Bishop being snatched, and I remember Les saying he'd pay a thousand dollars to get her back, but I don't remember saying I'd find her, and I sure as hell don't recall saying I'd take you with me."

Teresa put the plate on the table and shook the towel in his face as she shouted something in Spanish.

"I don't know exactly what you said, but I've got a feeling it wasn't too nice."

"I say that *Señor* Clay Best drinks too much tequila and he is a liar! That is what I say. After your friends left, you say you are going to find the *señorita* and that you wish me and Antonio to go. I asked Miguel to saddle our horses, and I pack for our trip, and now you say no? I think not *señor*, unless you want Teresa Romero to tell the world you are a liar!"

"Oh, Lord." Clay moaned, and leaned heavily in the doorway. "I don't recall none of that. Are you sure you just ain't making that part up? The part about me taking you along? No, I don't reckon you are," he added as she glared silently. "How am I supposed to take care of you and find Ruth at the same time?"

"I take care of myself, *señor*, so does Antonio. I can ride better than most men. I can shoot better than most men, and Diablo is a better horse than most horses."

"Well, I grant your hoss looks mighty fine from here, although Loco might want to argue some about your hoss being better. All I meant was, these things get kinda dangerous. How is this supposed to work? I can't be worrying about you and find Ruth Bishop at the same time."

"I take care of you while you find the *señorita*. That is how it works. There is nothing else."

"No, I don't reckon there is. The thing is, my head hurts too much to argue. Why don't I sleep this off, and we discuss it tomorrow? We'll both feel better then, and can talk some sense."

She spoke rapidly in Spanish and waved her towel at him once more. "We go now! You promised your friends, and you promised me. Doesn't your promise mean anything?"

"There's no way you're gonna let me out of this, are you? Didn't think so," he added as she shook her head. "You're as bad as June when she got riled, only worser. At least I could understand what June was saying. I speak a little Mexican, but not as fast as you. I ought to ride out of here and leave you to your own devices, but you'd probably sick that dog on me. Besides, I ain't never had any sense, or I wouldn't be in this fix in the first place."

He pointed a finger at her nose. "Okay, I'll try it for a day or two, but you do exactly like I say, or the deal's off. Got that?"

She nodded.

"I want us both to get out of this thing alive." He grabbed his gunbelt and struggled to get it buckled. "Although I ain't too sure I'll survive the trip to Cool Water in the condition I'm in."

Chapter 11

"This is where *Señora* Best is buried?"

"Yes, ma'am." Clay removed his hat and squatted on his heels beside June's grave.

"You loved her very much."

"Yes, ma'am, I still do. Her dying's left a big hole inside me. I can't seem to get it filled."

"*Si*, I know the feeling well." Teresa knelt on the opposite side of the grave and removed her flat-brimmed sombrero, then crossed herself as she began a rosary in Spanish. Clay rose and waited silently until the woman had finished her prayers.

"That was nice, ma'am. June would have appreciated it."

"*Gracias*. She was a great woman. I feel it in here." Teresa patted her breast before swatting the dust from her black skirt. She had Refugio's pistol tucked snugly into the belt which was fastened against her tiny waist.

"Yes, she sure was. I'm sure Refugio was also great in his own right. Now, let's see if we can't find Lester Bishop."

They led the horses across the road toward a wagon parked in front of the general store. A tumbleweed danced past them as a gust of hot wind slapped them in the face, and caused their eyes to sting. The majority of the buildings looked vacant. Clay felt a profound sadness at the lack of happy children who had once played in the street and begged cookies from June.

"*Carumba*, this is Cool Water? Where is the water, and where are the people, *señor?*"

"You're witnessing the death of a town. It's drying up, like everything else in Texas. It won't be long before Cool Water's only a memory."

He stopped as a man came from the back of the store carrying a heavy trunk which he slid into the wagon.

"Well, you're about the last person I expected to see around here, Clay. I guess it has something to do with Ruth?" The man wiped his palms against his pants before shaking Clay's hand.

"You got that right. Dusty and Utah hunted me down and said she'd been kidnapped."

"Run off, is more like it." A tall, thin woman came from the back of the store carrying a child's rocking horse. "No one forced her to go. She couldn't stand living with her grandfather after the way he treated Billy."

"Edith," the man cautioned.

"Oh, what's he going to do to us now, Harold? Fire you? We've already quit." She gave Clay a quick hug before backing away to eye Teresa. "Well, aren't you going to introduce us to your friend?"

"Oh, I plumb forgot my manners. This young lady is Teresa Romero. I've been renting a room at her place. That's where Dusty and Utah ran me down. Teresa, these folks are Harold and Edith Thomas. They run the Cool Water General Store."

"Not any more. We're pulling up stakes like everyone else around here. I can't sell nothing if there ain't no one to sell to," Harold said.

"Where are you folks headed?" Clay asked, as two small children carried a box of toys to the wagon.

"We aren't sure yet." Edith carefully put the small treasures into the buckboard. "We'll have to find work somewhere. Lester talked Harold into investing our entire savings into this business, and now it's gone."

"*Señora*, you may stay at my casa and rest for a few days when you reach Carrizo Springs. Tell Miguel at the stables Teresa Romero says it is okay. He will show you. It is a small casa, but it has water and a *baño*."

"She's right. It's small, but down right comfortable. Now, what can you tell me about Ruth Bishop," Clay asked.

"That's easy," Edith said as she drew closer. "Lester hired another marshal after you left. He was young and good-looking. Kind of flashy like Bill Mayfield, but not as nice. Billy might've been a scoundrel in a lot of ways, but everyone liked him. Well, this new fellow had an eye for Ruth, naturally, and she, hatin' her granddad so much for what he done, they took up together. It doesn't take good eyesight to see this town's dying, so it only took a few days before this flashy dresser up and quit, then Ruth disappeared a few days later. I say they run off together, and cooked up this scheme to get back at the old man."

"Huh, sounds reasonable. This new man have a name?"

"Rogers…Benjamin Rogers," Harold said. "He likes to talk and gamble. Causes a ruckus wherever he goes. He shouldn't be too hard to track down."

"Are any of Ruth's friends still around?"

"Sarah Walker and Louise Kirkland, but you'd better be quick if you want to ask them anything. Both of their families are pulling out tomorrow," Edith said.

"Yeah, I reckon. And I guess I ought to go over the particulars with Lester Bishop before I start on the wild-goose hunt. Do you know if he's home?"

"Sure, he's in his new home." Harold pointed toward the saloon. "That's where he spends most of his time these days."

"Thanks," Clay said, shaking their hands. "Maybe we'll run into each other again."

~ ~ ~

It took a few seconds for Clay's eyes to adjust to the dimness inside of the Cool Water Saloon. The place smelled of stale whiskey, tobacco and dust.

"It's about time you got here. What took so long?" Lester Bishop's voice boomed from a corner table at the far end of the saloon.

"I was out of town, and just got in last night. Keep a civil tongue, or I'm leaving the way I came in."

Lester was seated at the table with the two gunmen Clay knew as Curley and James Westfall. He didn't know much about Curley, but Westfall had been responsible for killing six men, and was touted as being quick-tempered and real quick to draw.

"Two beers, Charlie." Clay laid twenty cents on the counter.

"Yes sir, Clay. It's sure good to see you again. Are you and the young lady going to stick around for awhile?" The bartender slid two mugs of warm beer on the counter.

"No longer than we have to, Charlie."

Teresa tasted the sour brew and made a face before sliding the mug back onto the counter.

"Well, look what we've got here, Jim." Curley pushed back from the table and crossed the room toward Teresa. "A pretty Mex woman. She's too good for the likes of you, old man." He froze as Teresa jammed the muzzle of the .44 against his forehead and cocked the hammer. Curley's eyes bounced between the gun pressed against his head and the big dog growling at his feet.

Clay cocked his head to one side and grinned. He had been standing beside the woman and had not seen her pull the gun. "I wouldn't go pesterin' her none, if I were you. Not unless you figure on losing a fistful of brains. Teresa ain't just here for her looks. She rode with Bernal, and I seen her kill Joe Donaldson about two weeks ago over at Carrizo Springs. But, you can do what you want."

"Curly, get over here and sit down," Lester ordered. "Now, if you're ready, can we talk about my granddaughter?

Or, do you still want to waste more time while she's in the hands of kidnappers?"

"Well, I'll tell you what Les, Ruth is the *only* reason I'm here a'tall. 'Cause I see you ain't changed none, and I don't reckon you ever will. But before I go chasing all over Texas, I need some answers. The only thing I've got from Dusty and Utah is this note." He tossed the piece of paper on the table.

"Where are those two? They should have been back last night."

"Well, last night they was sitting at the same table with me and eating this woman's cooking. They said they ain't coming back here. The feller at the stable said they rode out early this morning, heading west. Now, tell me what this is all about."

"Somebody took Ruth, and I want her back. Now, stop wasting time and go get her!"

"Well, I'll just do that…as soon as I get some answers. I need something to go on. That note only says they want $25,000, and they will contact you. That ain't much to go on. Dusty said your housekeeper found the note Friday morning. Have you heard anything else?"

"No."

"Well, next question," Clay said with a snort. "Do you plan on paying the ransom?"

"Not unless I have to. It's your job to find her *before* the deadline," the old man growled.

"Well Les, Texas is a big place. Dimmit County's kind of big for that matter, with a million places to hide. I'll do what I can, but you'd best decide if you're gonna pay it before Tuesday rolls around. That's only three days from now, and that ain't very much time to search Texas for one girl.

"I'll start by questioning what folks are left in this town. I understand a couple of Ruth's friends are still here. I'll also need a recent picture of her, if you've got one, and a list of all the people she had any dealings with. Oh, I'll also need some expense money."

"Hell, I knew it would get around to money sooner or later," Lester growled. "How much are we talking about?"

"I'll ask around first, and see if I get any leads, then I'll let you know.

"Okay, I'll get the picture and make you a list. Then, I want you to get going. I'm not paying those bastards my hard-earned money to steal my granddaughter and cause me misery."

Chapter 12

"I don't like that man. He's not a nice person," Teresa said, as they unloaded the pack horse onto the porch of Clay's old house. The place was pretty much the way he'd left if after June had died.

"Most folks that meet Lester Bishop don't like him," Clay said. "I'll take the horses over to the stables and have Raul water and feed them." He cocked his head with a grin. "That is, if he's still here. I forgot to ask."

He led the horses to the south end of town, where he was pleased to find Maria busy making tortillas in front of her adobe house. She dropped what she was doing and ran to give him a hug. "Oh, *Señor* Clay. It is so good to see you again."

"And it's good to see you folks again. Is Raul around? I got some tired animals that need looking after." He stepped backward to dodge her three children as they raced past, chasing each other around in circles.

"*Si*, my husband will return in *un minuto*, and I will see he takes care of your horses. But you must eat with us, *señor*," Maria insisted.

"Well, I'd love to, but you see I've got a young woman back at the house who has sort of been looking after me."

"No! You got married again so soon?" Maria said with a laugh. "*Señor* Best, shame on you."

"No, no…it's nothing like that. I was renting a room at her place, and she had to tag along to make sure I found Ruth."

"*Si*, that is too bad what happened to her, no? Go bring the woman and we eat together. *Si*, there is plenty," she added as Clay started to protest. "Go bring her." She waved her hand, shooing him away.

~   ~   ~

Dinner with Raul and Maria Lopez had been a pleasant ending to an otherwise miserable day. Clay spread his blankets on his front porch and gazed at the stars as he pulled his boots off. He had started the day with a pounding headache, followed by a blazing hot and dusty ten-mile ride that ended with having to see Lester Bishop's sour face and hear his grating voice. He glanced at the Colt .45 and holster lying beside him. He still wondered what kept him from killing the man like he had promised himself he would do if he ever saw him again.

"*Señor* Best."

He turned to see her dressed in a thin cotton nightgown, standing in the doorway. Her body was silhouetted against the lamp on the dining room table.

"You are not sleeping inside the house? I make your bed for you, and I will sleep on the sofa."

"No, thank you, Teresa. I don't think I could stand sleeping in the same bed without her. Besides, it's cooler out here."

"*Bien*." She disappeared and returned seconds later to spread her blankets next to his. She laid Refugio's pistol next to her blankets. Then, locking her hands behind her head, she heaved a deep sigh.

"You are right, it is cooler outside. I feel the same way when Refugio died. I could not sleep in our bed either. I slept on the floor or with my grandmother. It will take you awhile *señor*. You will never forget your wife, and you will always love her, but the pain will finally go away. You will think of her and smile. Her memory will make you happy."

"Maybe."

"It will, I promise."

She was asleep minutes later, leaving Clay to his thoughts. Her dog had disappeared shortly after they left the saloon. Now it came trotting happily up on the porch. He stretched with a yawn and lay beside his mistress. The satisfied look on the dog's face gave Clay the impression that it had somehow eaten a nice dinner somewhere and visited a female in heat. Clay finally drifted off into a peaceful sleep and woke early with Teresa's body scrunched next to his.

Chapter 13

Clay spent several hours interviewing the few citizens who remained in Cool Water. His two best leads had come from Ruth's friends, Sarah Walker and Louise Kirkland. They told him that Ruth had been madly in love with Billy Mayfield, and couldn't forgive her grandfather for his part in Billy's death. Neither girl was surprised when Benjamin Rogers quit just a few days after being hired.

"There wasn't much for a Marshal to do around here anyway. As you can see, the town is almost dead. I can't wait to leave myself," Sarah said.

"Me neither," Louise said happily. "Pa says we're leaving first thing in the morning. I'm surprised anyone is staying."

"Do either of you know where Ruth might've gone?" Clay asked.

"Not really," Sara said as both girls shook their heads.

"We both think Ben came back that night to get her, and she left the note just to get Lester's goat," Louise said.

"And you've got no idea where they might've gone?"

"Not really. Ben used to brag about how popular he was in Dallas, but I really don't know," Sarah said sadly. "I miss her. Are you really going to bring her back here like Lester wants?"

Clay heaved a sigh. "That's what he's paying me for. But, if she's alright, and really happy, I'll more'n likely leave her alone. Anyone who's put up with that old goat as long as she has deserves a little peace."

~   ~   ~

"She ran away," Teresa said as she folded her clothes and packed them neatly inside one of the packs. She had fixed breakfast over an open fire, then bathed and washed her hair in June's metal washtub. Clay stared at her as he packed his pipe. Her black hair hung to her waist and glistened in the sunlight streaming through the window. She was downright pretty, although he couldn't figure why anyone would go to all the trouble scrubbing themselves clean, when they were going to fork a horse and ride a dusty trail in the blazing sun. It didn't make much sense.

"I figure it the same way. She probably ran off with that feller, and they're headed toward Dallas. Of course, there's always the chance they'll hang around and try to collect that ransom money before leaving."

Teresa finished packing and looked at her reflection in June's mirror as she carefully adjusted her sombrero. She tucked the .44 neatly into her belt, then grabbed her bag.

"Are you ready, *señor*?"

"Almost. We'd best have one final confab with Lester Bishop before riding out. Let me see that hogleg a minute."

"*Perdón?*"

"The pistol…Refugio's gun."

"Oh," she said with a nod.

Clay gave the weapon a once-over, inspecting it carefully and checking the action. "Confederate .44. Black powder cap and ball. Nice gun in its day. Seems like you and your husband took good care of it. How long since it's been emptied and reloaded?"

Teresa shrugged.

"We'd better do some target shooting when we leave town. A gun like this needs to be emptied and reloaded almost every day. If any moisture gets into the chambers, it'll misfire. Many a young soldier lost his life for that same reason. Here, try these."

Clay opened one of his bags and pulled out a black gunbelt with matching pistols. "I've go no use for these, but they're a might lighter than Refugio's pistol."

She sat on the edge of the bed studying the weapons, running her fingers across the shiny leather. She finally looked up at him with moist eyes.

"Billy?"

"You knew Bill Mayfield?" Clay drug his chair across the room and sat in front of her.

"*Si*, I know him. His brother, Rob, stay at my *casa*." Her accent thickened as she swiped at the tears on her cheeks. "Billy come and take Rob away. He says a man owes him much money, and he wanted him to help get it. They promise to come back, but they never did. Rob was supposed to help me with my restaurant."

"Ah-huh," Clay said with a nod. "You and Rob were good friends."

She nodded.

"Did you love him?"

"He was like my brother. I loved him very much, *Señor* Best. How do you get the guns? Is he dead?"

"Bill Mayfield? Yeah," Clay nodded slowly, "he got himself killed right out there in front of the bank, after he held it up. He's buried not too far from June. I'll show you before we leave town, if you want."

Teresa nodded and stared at the pearl-handled pistols once more. She wiped another teardrop that landed on the black leather. Clay rose silently and left her alone as he crossed the dusty street to talk to Lester Bishop. He had a feeling that Rob Mayfield had been more than a brother to Teresa Romero, but he suspected she would tell him the particulars in her own good time.

Chapter 14

The confab with Lester Bishop had been a waste of breath. The old skinflint was seated inside the saloon with James Westfall and Curley, drinking his breakfast. His only concerns were getting his granddaughter back, and keeping his money. After spending a few minutes listening to Lester rant, it seemed the money was a bigger concern than what condition Ruth was in.

"I'll find Ruth…one way or the other I'll find her. But, I'll need a little money to do it."

"How much money?" Lester glared across the table.

"Say, about five hundred ought to do it."

"Five hundred? Huh," the old man said with a laugh. "I only offered to pay you a thousand to find her. You haven't even left town yet. I'll give you three hundred, and not a penny more until you bring her back here." He reached into his coat and tossed a roll of bills on the table. "Understand me?"

"Yeah, Les, I understand you." Clay shoved the money into his pocket and turned away. He spoke over his shoulder as he headed toward the door.

"I'll let you know as soon as I find out something."

Clay crossed the dusty street at a brisk walk. He had almost reached the front porch when Teresa came out of the house carrying her bedroll. She glanced at him as she tied the roll to Diablo's saddle. She was dressed in a black silk blouse and a knee-length black riding skirt. The matching pearl-handled .38s stood out against her slender hips. The knee-high black boots were almost as shiny as the leather holsters, and the flat brimmed black sombrero had been carefully dusted.

"Is there something wrong, *señor*?"

"No." Clay smiled. "It's just that you look like you're fixing to ride in a parade, instead of hunt down a kidnapped girl."

"This is how I wish to look today, *señor*." She swung into the saddle and glared down at him. "Are you ready, or should I unpack?"

"Oh Lord." Clay heaved a sigh and ran his huge hand across his face. Finding Ruth Bishop was going to be tough enough, without having to put up with a woman's sudden change in moods.

"No, I'm more'n ready. I thought you wanted to see where Bill Mayfield's buried."

"I find his grave and say prayers while you are in the cantina. Let's go." She gave him a stern glare before nudging Diablo with her heels.

Clay watched her trot the red horse toward the edge of town before mounting Loco. He gave the dog a stern look. "You'd best quit lying in the shade and shaking your tail, Antonio. She's liable to get peeved at you for something you've done. And don't ask me what it was I did, 'cause I don't know. I don't think it matters."

~   ~   ~

Clay set a leisurely pace, walking the horses as he scanned the desert for signs. He finally gave up the hope of ever finding tracks. Anything left by Ruth Bishop and Benjamin Rogers had been completely destroyed by a combination of Lester's cowboys searching for her, and the dry wind blowing dust and sand. They rode for several hours in silence, heading in a northwest direction that would take them past Carrizo Springs. Clay actually preferred the silence, since it gave him time to mull things over, and consider the facts from different angles. Conversation and idle talk always confused things and got people into trouble. He'd seen lawmen completely miss something in plain sight, simply because they had their lips flapping in the breeze, or were listening to some senseless talk. They descended into a dry arroyo where Clay turned aside and dismounted.

"Is something wrong, *señor*?"

"No, I just figured it was time to get acquainted with our company." He pulled the Winchester from its scabbard and patted Loco on the rump.

"*¿Qué?*" She dropped to the ground and grabbed the reins to all three horses.

"Yep, they've been following us since we left Cool Water. See?" He motioned toward the small cloud of dust a quarter of a mile back. "They've been keeping pace with us, like they are waiting for something. I just never liked folks following me, unless I know what they're up to."

"*Si.*" Teresa pulled the horses to one side and tied them to a hunk of driftwood, then scampered back to kneel behind a bush about six feet to Clay's right. She checked the loads in both pistols before sliding the sombrero to the back of her head. Clay nodded silently. The woman was familiar with the drill.

The dust cloud drew closer as beads of sweat collected on their brows and trickled down their necks. Dark circles of moisture grew on Teresa's blouse as she watched the riders approach.

"They are the same hombres from the cantina. Why do they follow us?"

"I'm carrying $300." Clay cocked the rifle. The two men veered toward a gradual incline in the bank, then entered the arroyo twenty-five yards or more north of where Clay and Teresa were shielded by a bend in the channel. They then exited the opposite side of the arroyo.

"They did not see us," Teresa said in a hoarse whisper.

"Maybe. We'd best wait a minute and see." Clay scampered to where the men had climbed the bank and peered over the top. They were heading toward the abandoned church north of Carrizo Springs.

"I guess maybe I was wrong. They might not have been interested in us, or the $300. Could be they've got another ace up their sleeve." He grabbed the canteen from Loco and tossed it to Teresa. "I figure we'd best follow, and see what they're up to."

"*¿Qué?*" She took a swallow and passed the canteen back to Clay.

"Because men like Curley and Westfall don't take leisurely rides in this kind of heat for nothing. They're up to something. I just don't know what." He took a swallow from the canteen and checked Loco's cinches.

They followed the men a quarter of a mile or so back, staying mostly to the brush. Curly and James Westfall passed the old church and swung into Carrizo Springs from the west end of town. Clay stopped to study the situation as perspiration dripped from under his hat and landed on the saddle.

"I reckon we'd best get in out of this heat, but I don't figure on letting anyone know we're anywhere near Carrizo Springs until we see what those two are up to."

"Maybe they come to watch the chapel, and see who comes to get the money."

"Could be, but I ain't buying it. Men like them are always up to something no good."

Chapter 15

Clay and Teresa spent the night at the stables. Miguel put the tired horses in one of the back stalls where no one was likely to see them, and promised to let them know if Curley or Westfall left town.

"No need to worry, *Señor* Best. My Juanita's brother plays the guitar at the cantina, and I will tell him to watch the *hombres* for you. He will do this, or Juanita will not cook for him, and he will be eating in the cantina and die. Besides, I have their horses. See?" He pointed toward the corral, where one of his sons was rubbing down two lathered mustangs. "I will know when they are leaving and let you know."

"Sounds reasonable. I'll take you at your word, Miguel.

Miguel sent two of his six children to the stable with plates of beans, tortillas and beefsteaks smothered in salsa. Clay sat down next to Teresa when she heaved a big sigh.

"Did you kill Guillermo?"

"Who? Bill Mayfield?"

"*Si*, did you kill him?"

"Lord no. So, that's what's been bothering you?" Clay shook his head and chuckled. "Billy didn't need killing, but he needed to be taught a lesson. Besides, I knew enough to know that Lester Bishop did owe him a wad of money. Billy came into town that morning to rob the bank, but I'd already gotten wind of it, and had deputized three of his friends. We were going to catch him red-handed, then haul his carcass off to Austin to turn him over to Judge Keller. I know the man personally, and figured I could talk him into giving Bill a swift kick in the britches to straighten him out." Clay took a bite of steak and chewed thoughtfully.

"What happened then?"

"Well, the Lipperts happened, and all hell broke loose."

Teresa heaved another sigh and refilled their cups with wine. "You talk in circles. What are these Lipperts?"

"I just kind of figured everyone knew what happened. I guess you didn't, did you?"

She shook her head.

"Well, let's see. They were three brothers, who claimed Billy had killed a fourth brother of theirs over a card game, and they figured on settling the score. They spied Billy's horse in front of the bank, and jumped right into the thick of things before I could stop 'em. They braced Bill as he came out of the bank. Billy killed one of them, and the other two did for him. They also killed one of my deputies before I could stop them. That's how come I got those guns."

"What happened to Rob? Is he buried near Guillermo? I did not see his grave."

"Rob? No, I'm sorry," Clay said with a soft laugh and gave her wrist a gentle squeeze. "Rob wasn't even there. He and Billy had themselves a difficulty, and Rob showed up late that afternoon, all buggered up. It was a good thing too, or he might've gotten himself killed too. Last I seen of him, he was heading back to see some girl named Clara Jean. The way he was talking, I kind of figure they might've gotten married by now."

"*Si*," she said with a smile, and took a sip of wine, "he told me about her. *Gracias* for telling me." She took a bite of tortilla and chewed thoughtfully.

Clay finished his beans and sopped the plate clean with the last tortilla. Teresa seemed content with his recollection of Bill and Rob Mayfield, and said little as she spread their bedrolls on fresh hay inside an empty stall. The woman was a mystery to him. She had more twists and turns than a Comanche trail through the Anacacho Mountains. He also figured he had enough on his mind trying to find Ruth Bishop, without trying to figure out Teresa Romero. He decided to tell her to stay home in the morning, where she belonged, and give up the notion of chasing after him and getting in his way. He tossed that idea aside as the woman sat on the bench to clean and oil the Smith and Wesson .38s. She finished, and grabbed a few things before disappearing toward the outhouse.

Clay cleaned and oiled his own guns, then pulled his boots off and lay back on his bedroll. Teresa finally returned, looking clean and fresh. She knelt in the corner of the stall, crossed herself and said her prayers, clutching a tiny crucifix on a chain around her neck. She finally blew out the lamp and wished him a goodnight. He woke at dawn with her hair tickling his nose. She had scooted next to him during the night, and had her right arm draped across his chest.

Chapter 16

They spent the majority of the day staying out of sight, waiting for Westfall and Curley to do something. The men seemed content to spend their time at the cantina drinking, playing cards and pestering the women who worked in the back rooms. According to Miguel's brother in law, both men spent the night with the women and rose late in the day. It wasn't until late in the afternoon that Miguel motioned for them to hide in the back room. Clay and Teresa peeked through the partially opened door as the two drunken men staggered into the stables. They paid their bill and Miguel had his oldest son saddle their horses. Curley needed help climbing into the saddle, then the two trotted their horses behind the cantina and out of the town the way they had come.

Clay paid their bill as Teresa packed. Juanita brought a small package of hot tortillas, jerked beef, dried fruit and a bottle of brandy. They rode out of town just minutes behind the men, keeping them in sight, but far enough away to stay out of trouble. Curley and Westfall dismounted near the church and tied their horses in a thicket of mesquite.

Clay and Teresa crouched behind a greasewood plant. "What are they doing?" Teresa whispered in Clay's ear as she peered over his left shoulder.

"Picking up where they left off in town, with a bottle. Today's the day Lester's supposed to pay the ransom, and I figure they're supposed to be keeping watch, in case some idgit's dumb enough to come looking for the money. Thing is, both of them are too drunk to see a brass band in a parade, if one happened by. You and me had best make ourselves comfortable and see what happens."

They made a dry camp, shielded by a clump of greasewood, then ate their dinner of corn tortillas, beef jerky and dried fruit, washing it down with water from a canteen. The men laughed and grew louder as darkness fell. They even built a small fire.

"They are *loco en la cabeza*," Teresa grumbled lowly. "People will see that fire and hear them from far off. The men who stole the girl will not come for the money."

"You got that right, sister. I might as well smoke my pipe. It won't make no difference." He shielded the glow of the match under his hat as he lit the pipe. "Besides," he said, taking a puff, "I've got my doubts that anyone was coming to collect the money anyway."

"*¿Qué?*" She turned around to stare at him.

Clay leaned back against his saddle and drew thoughtfully on the pipe.

"June and me knew Ruth pretty well, and the girl spent quite a bit of time helping June around the house, especially when she was having one of her spells. Ruth Bishop was one of the prettiest, kindest, gentlest girls you'd ever meet. I doubt that she'd hold up her skinflint grandpa for $25,000, no matter how peeved she got. I've never liked this deal from the beginning. Someone's left a joker in the deck."

"You talk in riddles again, *señor*."

"What I mean is, them two sharing that bottle over there are somehow tied up in this whole thing. I just ain't figured it all out yet. I figure Ruth might've run off with that handsome devil, but someone else left that note."

Teresa squatted on her heels beside Clay and nodded thoughtfully. "So, what do we do now, *Señor* Best?"

"We sit here and wait just like we're doing, and see if we can't figure what them two yahoos are up to. Nothing's gonna happen tonight with them carrying on. I don't think they believed anything was gonna happen either, or they wouldn't be acting like a couple of fools. Westfall's been down a trail or two, and he ain't stupid. He knows no one's coming, and he's got something up his sleeve. So, we just wait. You could pour us a little of that brandy, if you had a mind to. We might as well enjoy ourselves as much as we can."

A cool breeze swept through the brush, chasing the blistering heat of the day toward the south. Teresa spread their bedrolls on the sand and removed her boots. She snuggled under her blankets and dozed off, leaving Clay to take the first watch. Antonio perked up his ears as a coyote howled somewhere to the east, and was answered seconds later by another toward the west. Clay scratched the dog's ears, calming him down. Curley and Westfall drank themselves into a stupor, snoring loudly as their fire died down. Clay woke Teresa around 1:00 and removed his own boots. The men were still snoring. Clay paused with one of his boots in his hand when Curley staggered to his feet. Teresa gave Clay a disgusted look as the drunk stumbled toward them. He paused about halfway toward where she and Clay were camped and made water.

Teresa mumbled something about a stupid pig as the man stumbled back toward his bedroll. Clay rolled over and fell asleep, satisfied that nothing more was going to happen.

Chapter 17

Ruth Bishop stood next to Ranger Hart as she watched the crude pine box being lowered into the freshly dug grave. There were three other people who had taken the time to attend the graveside ceremony for Benjamin Rogers: The two men who had been hired to dig and refill the grave, and the local minister. He had just read from the book of Psalms and said a prayer, requesting God to be merciful when the books on Ben were tallied. Ruth had reason to doubt that the Good Lord would heed that prayer. Her freshly bruised right cheek was a reminder of Ben's true character. He had given her that one at Lehmann's Ranch when she asked about the wire from Curley and Jim Westfall.

"That's none of your goddamn business," he had said as he hit her with his fist. He had then taken the last of her money from her purse and slammed the door. She hadn't spoken a word to him since that incident. Not that there would have been time for conversation. He had gotten himself killed inside the saloon over a stupid card game, exactly three hours later. Ruth hated to admit it, but she actually felt relieved when the drunken weasel was lowered into his grave. Her only fear now was what to do about her own situation.

She had taken up with Benjamin Rogers after Clay Best had ridden out of Cool Water. June and Clay had been her only true allies in town. They understood and listened to her when she cried on their shoulders. She had friends her own age who loved her; Sarah Walker and Louise Kirkland had been like sisters to her. But even close friends don't always keep everything secret, and they sometimes don't understand when you tell them how you really feel. Sarah had always envied Ruth, and said how lucky she was to have such a rich grandfather who bought her pretty clothes. How do you tell someone that you are really a prisoner? Now June and Clay Best, who were the closest thing she had to a mother and father, were both gone and she was alone.

After her mother had died, three years earlier, she had thought coming to live with her rich grandpa Lester would be a good idea. She was an only child, and had spent her early childhood on a military base, where her army-sergeant father had been stationed. Ruth remembered how proud she had been when her father, Leland, would don his blue dress uniform with its golden braids and shiny saber. He was a loving father who adored his daughter. When Ruth turned twelve, her father's unit was transferred from Fort Duncan to Fort Inge to help settle an Indian uprising. He had planned to send for her and her mother once he got settled. They instead received word that Sergeant Leland Bishop had been killed by Lipan-Apache during a raid on a small settlement near Uvalde.

Her Grandpa Lester attended his son's funeral, but remarked later that Leland Rogers' entire career in the Army had been a waste. He believed his son should have gone into the cattle business and gotten rich like his father. The fact that her grandfather had offered little help to her and her mother in the remaining years of her mother's life should have given Ruth a clue as to the man's character.

Lester Bishop claimed to love his granddaughter, and dressed her in the finest clothing money could buy. He hired private tutors to make sure her education was complete. But he paraded her around like an object, especially while entertaining important people involving business deals. She had been told repeatedly what a loving and generous grandfather Lester was, and she was lucky to have him to take care of her. Folks meant well, but what no one realized was the generosity only amounted to what Lester thought would be to his own benefit.

The pretty clothes were for her to wear when he said she could wear them. Then he would personally choose which dress and which hat she wore on a particular occasion, whether she liked them or not. The rest of the time she was to wear simple house dresses, for fear of spoiling the fancy clothes inside her wardrobe. The education was also for display at his choosing. She had made the mistake of not being charming to a particular guest she disliked and received Grandpa Lester's wrath later for her disobedience. She tried to explain that she did not like the fat, vulgar man, and found him repulsive, but that didn't matter. It didn't even matter when she told her grandfather the man had made suggestive remarks while he was out of the room, and had even tried putting his hands on her. What mattered to Lester Bishop was that the man represented a potential business transaction where he stood to make thousands of dollars.

Grandpa Lester also chose her diet. He wanted her to remain rail-thin and attractive, which meant she had spent the past three years feeling hungry. And she was supposed to keep out of the sun as much as possible to maintain her pale complexion.

Then her grandfather hired Billy Mayfield. She was instantly drawn to the flashy cowboy toting matching pearl-handled pistols on his hips. He was educated, at least by Texas standards, and could quote poetry as well as read and write. He was witty, and won the hearts of most anyone he met, especially hers. Ruth fell madly in love with Billy the first time he smiled at her.

"I didn't take you in and then spent hundreds of dollars on your education and clothing, so that you could take up with a hired hand. I forbid you to see Bill Mayfield again. Do you understand me?" Lester had said.

Ruth was afraid her grandpa might discharge Billy and she would never see him again, so they agreed to keep their romance a secret. They met in the middle of the night while her grandfather was sleeping, or when he happened to be away on business. She knew Billy had been with other women, and was certainly no angel. He drank some, and she'd heard him cuss more than once. But Billy had plans, and those plans included her. She loved him terribly, and knew beyond a shadow of a doubt that he loved her just as much. The fact that he had come back for her was witness to his love.

Grandpa Lester had discharged Billy Mayfield after a drunken card game inside the Cool Water Saloon, in which her grandpa had lost a sizable amount of money to Billy. Dusty and several of Billy's friends had told her later that Billy warned Lester not to keep increasing the pot. He even tried walking away from the table. But her grandfather was drunk and would not listen to reason, so he went as far as ordering Billy back to the table. When the game was over, he owed Billy more than five-thousand dollars. The enraged man refused to pay and ordered Billy off his property.

Billy had come back last fall after he knew her grandfather had sold a small herd of cattle. He asked her grandfather for the money and was again ordered off the property. He threatened to have Billy killed if he ever showed up again. Billy sent word through a mutual friend to be ready to leave. He planned to come in the middle of the night and they would run as far from Cool Water as they could go. He was going to take her to New Orleans. Instead, Billy had been shot and killed in front of her grandfather's bank. Grandpa Lester said Billy had been killed while robbing the bank, and had gotten exactly what he deserved. He ordered her not to attend Billy's funeral, but she had shown up anyway, and wept bitterly as his body was lowered into the ground. That was when she started hating her grandfather.

~   ~   ~

"May I join you?"

Ruth was sipping a cup of coffee with Ranger Hart inside Edith's Café, when the well-dressed, lanky man approached their table. She guessed him to be in his early thirties. He was certainly not handsome by any stretch of her imagination, but he seemed pleasant enough, and his smile revealed a set of perfectly formed teeth.

"Certainly," Ranger Hart said, jumping to his feet as he shook the man's hand. "Judge Stanley, I'd like you to meet Mrs. Rogers. Ruth this is Judge Buford Stanley. He's a circuit judge, and he's here to try the Walker brothers. Ruth and I just came from burying her husband. I was about to ask her what her plans are now."

"I am pleased to meet you, Your Honor." Ruth offered her hand.

"Please, call me Buford, and the pleasure is all mine." The judge took her fingers and bowed his head slightly. "When I arrived yesterday I saw you crossing the street with a fellow. I didn't know he was your husband, until someone told me it was the same gentleman who got killed inside the saloon. Is that true?"

"Yes, I'm afraid so," Ruth said.

"May I offer my condolences," he said. "I hope he wasn't the one who gave you that bruise on you cheek."

"Yes, I'm afraid he did do that. I don't believe Benjamin was the man I thought he was when I first met him."

"I'm sorry to hear that," the judge said.

"Do you have any idea what you plan to do now, Mrs. Rogers?" Ranger Hart asked.

"Actually, no I don't." Ruth added extra cream to her coffee and stirred slowly. "I can't go back to Cool Water. I left because I felt as if I was being suffocated, and my grandfather would kill me if I showed up now…after running away with Benjamin." She dropped the spoon into her saucer and shook her head as a single tear trickled down her cheek. "I actually believed he loved me. Both of my parents are dead, so I don't have anyone to turn to. I am educated, so perhaps I can find a job doing something. But..." she covered her mouth as several more tears spilled over, "I am nineteen, and alone. I will kill myself before I work in a saloon or house of ill repute." She shrugged and smiled weakly. "That is my situation, gentlemen. So frankly…no, I have no idea what I am going to do."

Chapter 18

Clay woke at dawn to see Teresa huddled against her saddle, wrapped tightly in a blanket with only her face exposed. She whispered "good morning" and he sat a silent moment studying her, realizing how pretty she actually was, and wishing there was some way of capturing that picture. He instead mumbled "mornin'" as he pulled on his boots and jammed his hat down on his head. He then stretched and buckled his gunbelt. It was time to go to work.

Clay motioned for her to follow as he slipped silently away from camp, circling to the back of the abandoned church. The back door was completely missing, and the sound of tiny feet scurrying across the stone floor greeted him as he crept inside. Teresa hesitated at the door.

"What are we doing, *Señor* Best?"

"We're checking to see if the ransom was paid, but we'd best be quiet while we're doing it. Our friends might mistake us for the kidnappers and bore a hole in our hides. Look around and see if anything looks like it might contain money."

Clay searched the back room as Teresa entered the main sanctuary. She quickly poked her head back inside.

"*Señor* Best, come," she motioned, "is this what we are looking for?" She pointed toward a canvas bag sitting in the middle of the floor. Clay squatted on his heels and pushed his hat to the back of his head as he read the lettering on the bag.

"Bank Of Cool Water. Yeah, I reckon it is. Better keep an eye out for our friends. We don't want them interrupting us." Teresa moved closer to a window and peered toward the drunken gunmen sleeping in the brush.

"Well, that solves one mystery," Clay said with a chuckle. He brought the sack to the window and held it for her to examine.

"There is only a little money on top. The rest is paper." She let the stack of bills fall back into the bag. "He did not pay for his own granddaughter? *Carumba!*"

"I told you he doesn't part with money too easy. This bag was supposed to be bait, and those two out there were supposed to kill whoever came to get it. Now, we'd best be getting back before they decide to do us in, and claim we're the ones who wrote that note."

Clay replaced the money carefully on top of the paper and positioned the bag exactly as they had found it. They left the same way through the rear door, and circled back to their camp. They were finishing a breakfast of beef jerky, cold tortillas and dried fruit when Westfall staggered to his feet to relieve himself against the side of the church. Teresa shook her head and called down several curses in Spanish as Curley joined him.

"*Jesus Cristo* will not like them doing that to his church."

"I reckon not," Clay agreed.

It took several minutes and several swallows from a fresh bottle before the men were fit to saddle their horses. Curley retrieved the canvas bag from the church and the men laughed as they rode away.

"*Santa Maria, Señor* Best. I do not understand these men."

"Well," Clay paused to take a swallow from his canteen and passed it to Teresa, "they knew no one was coming. I figure they were in on this deal from the beginning. They'll go back and tell Lester that whoever it was came and discovered he was dealing from the bottom of the deck. They might even claim whoever it was had Ruth with them, and had a gun pointed toward her head. I'm guessing they'll say the kidnappers are now demanding even more money. They'll keep at it until he gives in, then they'll take the money and run. That's what I think. Now, all we've got to do is prove it."

"How are we going to do that, *señor*?" Teresa finished rolling her bedroll and stared at him.

"The only way I know is to find Ruth Bishop. She's the key to this whole thing. Without finding her, we're left holding the joker. We'll waste our time looking and figuring, and won't have anything to show for it. Thing is," he gave the cinch on Loco's saddle a tug, "Texas is a mighty big state to be looking for one girl."

"Then, we'd better get looking." She quickly tied her bedroll to the back of her saddle.

"I reckon. But let's head back into Carrizo Springs first. I could stand a strong cup of coffee."

Chapter 19

They traveled north and camped at Comanche Creek late that afternoon. Teresa added chunks of dried beef to a pan of canned beans and heated them with corn tortillas over a campfire while Clay attended to the horses. Zavala County was mostly brush land, crisscrossed by dry streambeds. The thick, short grass and mesquite were ideal for cattle, and normally thrived on the hot summer sun and a winter rainfall totaling more than twenty-one inches. The area had once been thick with buffalo, but the hiders had all but made the animals extinct. Even the bear was getting harder to find. Antelope and whitetail deer now mingled with thousands of head of long-horned cattle. Clay had also seen several javelinas and coyotes that day, as well as a few rabbits. Turkeys and quail could readily be found hiding among oak, elm and hackberries growing beside the streams. Ash, pecan and persimmon trees were also thick. Clay paused with Loco's saddle in his hands and gazed around, wondering what had made him give up ranching as a youth to become a lawman. This part of Texas was the perfect area to raise cattle.

~ ~ ~

The Cross S Ranch covered 10,000 acres of south Zavala County, and dipped slightly into Dimmit County. The discovery of several artesian wells only a year earlier had begun to change things rapidly. While the crystal-clear water spewing ice-cold from the ground seemed ideal for cattle and wildlife, there was already talk of developers wanting to buy the Cross S as well as several other ranches. They wanted to subdivide the ranches into smaller, ten-acre plots and build a city. One of them had mentioned calling the town Crystal City after the artesian wells. Clay didn't cotton to the idea much. In the first place, ten acres wasn't enough land to raise anything other than a couple of cows and a passel of children. Besides, he figured the last thing they needed was another town. He liked things the way they were. He was beginning to wonder if men like him might become extinct like the buffalo some day. They crossed a wooden bridge and rode up to the main house as a woman in a blue housedress and white apron tossed a pan of dishwater into the yard.

"Well howdy, Clay. I ain't seen you around in awhile. Who's your friend?"

"Howdy yourself, Rosie." Clay dismounted and shook her hand. He glanced up at Teresa who was still in the saddle, staring at the woman. "Well, get down, she won't bite." He waited until Teresa was standing beside him before making the introductions.

"Rosie, this is Teresa Romero. Teresa, this is Rosie Maze. She and her husband sort of run this ranch and take care of things for the owner."

"*Buenos días, señora.*" Teresa offered her hand, but Rosie wiped her palm on her apron before taking it.

"Mrs. Romero is trying to help me locate a missing girl," Clay said as the woman eyed him.

"Oh," she gave a nod, "I heard about June's passing, and figured you might have found a new way of grieving."

"No, just business, Rosie."

"That's good. 'Cause I was gonna slap a knot up-beside your head if you was turning out like some of them other fellas. The men have gone off to discuss business with them city developers, and I don't know when they'll be coming back. Come on inside and I'll make a fresh pot of coffee.

I've got a pan of cornbread in the oven and a pot of elk stew on the stove. I shot the critter yesterday when he was eating out of my garden. Violet and me was fixing to sit down and have us a bowl. Y'all are more than welcome to join us. There's plenty."

"They ain't gonna sell off so they can build a town here, are they?" Clay asked as he stomped the dust from his boots.

"Heck if I know. They never tell us women anything. We're always the last to know."

~   ~   ~

They had finished eating and were sipping coffee when Clay passed Ruth's picture to Rosie and her daughter.

"Yes, I remember seeing her about four or five days ago," Rosie said thoughtfully as she packed tobacco into a corncob pipe. Teresa was transfixed by the woman who dipped snuff and smoked a pipe like a man. She knew several Mexican women who smoked tailor-made cigarettes, and a few others who rolled their own. There was one she had met in Piedras Negras who smoked cigars, but she knew of none who smoked and dipped at the same time. She herself had taken a couple of puffs from one of Refugio's cigarettes, but it made her cough, and she did not like it.

"Only she wasn't calling herself Ruth Bishop. She was with some fancy-dressed fella, and she was calling herself Mrs. Rogers. I'll tell you what, he thought pretty well of himself. I didn't think he was any big shucks myself." She struck a match and blew small clouds of smoke into the air.

Violet smiled warmly at Teresa as she refilled her cup with fresh coffee.

"Papa don't like her dipping or smoking, but he can't get her to quit."

"He ain't likely gonna, either. Not until he puts me in a box and buries me in the back yard. And I want my pipe and tobacco tin in the box with me when that time comes."

"Huh," Clay said thoughtfully. "I didn't know they'd gotten hitched."

"I didn't see no ring on her finger, but I can't swear to it either way." Rosie snorted.

"Do you know where they went?" Clay asked.

"I can't say exactly where they were going," Violet replied, "but they were heading west, toward the Mexican border. They were traveling by buggy, so they'll have to stick to the roads."

"Well actually, that little bit of information is downright helpful," Clay said. He drained the last of his coffee and stood.

"Thanks for the vittles, Rosie. They were tasty as usual, but we'd best be going. Tell that knob-head husband I'm sorry I missed him, and if they decide to sell off this place to them developers, I'll come and shoot him in the knee."

"I certainly will. Sure you don't wanna spend the night?"

"No, Les Bishop ain't gonna pay us unless we find his granddaughter. So we'd best git."

~ ~ ~

"Where do we go now, *Señor* Best?" They had ridden a mile, following the road due west before Teresa broached the subject.

"I don't rightly know. But I'm guessing they either headed toward La Pryor or Eagle Pass. If the feller she's run off with is tied up in this mess with Curley and Westfall, he ain't likely to get too far from all that money, especially if he thinks of himself as a flashy gambler."

"Do you think *Señorita* Bishop is involved also?"

"Ain't likely. She probably thinks she's in love, and mostly wanted to get shed of her grandpa. Let's head to Eagle Pass. It's larger, and a hell-roarin' hole right on the Rio Grande."

Chapter 20

Eagle Pass lay approximately thirty-five miles due west of The Cross S Ranch. Clay and Teresa made a dry camp among a clump of greasewood and cactus, and took turns keeping watch. They were on the trail early the following morning and were nearing Eagle Pass when they were overtaken by a group of seven riders. The young, dust-covered man in the lead drew up and flashed Clay a grin.

"Howdy Clay, what got you out of your comfortable office, and out here?"

"Howdy yourself, Ira. First off, it wasn't so comfortable, and second, I quit working for Lester Bishop." He turned toward Teresa and motioned toward the men.

"This jasper is Ira Aten, and these characters call themselves Texas Rangers." He turned back toward the rangers. "And this lady is Teresa Romero, so y'all had best mind your manners."

"We sure can do that, Clay, but what's June gonna think of you being out here with a good-looking woman by your lonesome?"

The grin on Clay's face disappeared. "June's dead, Ira. She died almost five months ago."

"Aw Jesus, Clay, I'm real sorry to hear that. She was a real Texas lady."

"Sure was," one of the men agreed as several others nodded.

"Much obliged," Clay said. "I know she was too good for the likes of me. As to why we're out here, Mrs. Romero was renting me a room in Carrizo Springs, when we somehow got roped into looking for Lester's granddaughter. It looks like someone might've made off with her, and Les got a ransom note for $25,000. Have y'all seen hide or hair of this young lady?" He dismounted and dug Ruth's photograph from his saddlebag, then handed it to Ira. The ranger shrugged and passed it to the others. The third man nodded.

"Yeah, sure, I seen her early this morning, back at Lehmann's Ranch. You remember," he said to Ira, "I ran into the post office to see if there were any messages?"

"Yeah." Ira nodded.

"She was with a big feller with blond hair and moustache, and they were having one hell of a row right there in front of the door. According to Frank Lehmann, that man she's married to likes to buck the tiger. Frank said some new fellow rolled in awhile back, who used to deal faro back in Natchez, Mississippi, and set up a table inside The Lucky Seven. According to Frank, her husband parked himself at the faro table last night and lost their entire poke. Anyway, they were going at it tooth-and-nail when I got there. They're staying at Louise's Boarding House. I can take you to them, after we finish this little chore of ours." He shrugged and handed Ruth's picture back to Clay.

"Speaking of which, we'd best get going," Ira said, and gave Clay a crooked grin. "Now, that the Texas Rangers have found your fugitives, you're welcome to tag along and watch how real lawmen catch desperados."

"I reckon we can do that, if Wayne will take me to Ruth like he says he can. What are we looking for? A couple of chicken-thieves?"

Chapter 21

The rangers were looking for horse thieves that had been prowling the larger ranches along the Rio Grande Valley and driving prized stock into Mexico. Appeals sent to Webb County Sheriff Dario Gonzales had brought great promises but no action, let alone any posse, and the horse stealing continued. Old Dario, as the disgusted ranchers called him, was the kingpin of a corrupt political ring ruling the area, and he also directed an inner council nicknamed The Forty Thieves. Citizens suspected Dario of receiving a percentage of all the stolen stock, but no one had been able to prove it. The angry ranchers had finally called on the Texas Rangers to put a stop to the horse stealing. Although Lieutenant Ira Aten was only in his mid twenties, he was already a seasoned veteran, and had been well schooled in dealing with horse thieves, rustlers, and murderers.

One of the ranchers had discovered some of his stock missing that very morning. The patrol came across hoof prints of a small herd of horses about midday, south of Eagle Pass.

"Think they're our rustlers, Ira?" Wayne asked as the lieutenant examined the tracks.

"Most likely, and these tracks are fresh. They're bound for the Rio Grande, so we'd better rustle."

They followed the trail at a full gallop and crested a small rise minutes later, revealing the small herd of stolen horses and five rustlers ahead.

The thieves had already crossed Ambrosio Creek, and one turned in his saddle to see the charging posse. He yelled, and the men abandoned the horses, riding furiously toward a high, rugged peak overlooking Old Mexico.

"At 'em, boys!" yelled Ira. "Head 'em off before they hit the border."

Teresa lashed Diablo as Clay rode away. The magnificent horse pulled beside Loco and kept pace with him as they plunged across the stream. Three of the rangers' horses bogged down in a pocket of deep mud and fell, pitching their riders. Ranger Griffin cried out in pain as his horse fell on him, smashing his collarbone. Frank Sieker righted his pony and joined the others as they charged up the hill.

Diablo sprinted ahead. Halfway up the hill Teresa overtook the bandits and rode straight toward them, with Clay close behind, yelling for her to stop. Teresa continued her charge until she was close enough to touch the nearest rustler. She pulled Diablo to a halt and pointed one of the pistols at the man as she shouted.

"Alto! We are Texas Rangers, and you are under arrest." The rustler raised his rifle and shot her from the saddle.

"Ahhgh!" Clay yelled as he fired his Winchester. He levered the gun quickly and shot the man a second time before he fell. The rustlers turned their guns on the rangers. Ira was firing his Winchester from horseback as rapidly as he could. One of his bullets ripped through an outlaw's shoulder and he dropped his rifle. The man leaned over the horse and gripped the mane as he tried to escape, but the rustlers were surrounded in seconds, and the shooting died as quickly as it had started.

Clay leaped from his saddle and ran toward Teresa. The woman was clutching a bloody blouse as tears streamed from the corner of her eyes.

"Oooh, *Santa Maria, Señor* Clay. It hurts so bad!"

"I reckon it does. Just lie back and let me have a look." Clay unbuttoned her blouse. The .44 slug had ripped through her chest high, above her right breast, and exited through her back.

"Aw, Lordy," Ira said as he knelt beside them. "Wayne, grab the medical kit. We've got a couple of rangers down. This woman's hit pretty bad."

"Is it really bad, *Señor* Best? Am I going to die?" she asked in a raspy voice.

"Naw, just a scratch. This idgit don't know what he's talking about. Just relax."

"It hurts!"

"I know it does, but we're gonna patch you up and get you to the nearest doctor."

Clay glanced up at Wayne as he opened the kit.

"You gotta stop the bleeding."

"I'll do my best, Clay, but a .44 leaves a pretty big hole."

Chapter 22

"You really didn't have to go to all this trouble, Mr. Stanley. To be honest, I really don't know why you are being so nice to me." Ruth smiled at the judge seated across the table as she sipped her water. When Judge Buford Stanley had asked her to have dinner with him that evening, she had thought they would either be eating at Edith's Café or the boarding house. But he instead had asked permission to have a private table in a remote corner of the patio behind Frank Lehmann's ranch house, where he had been staying as a guest.

Judge Stanley waited until the Lehmann's housekeeper poured the wine before answering.

"I know I didn't have to do anything, Miss Bishop, but I wanted to be alone with you. To be very honest, I was quite taken with you the first time I saw you, and I haven't been able to get you out of my mind. It was really hard to keep focused during the trial."

"That brings up something I've been dying to ask you. Does it bother you to sentence someone to be hanged, like you did this afternoon? I know those two men were evil…but still, you will be responsible for having them executed."

"I didn't sentence them to death, Miss Bishop. They sentenced themselves by choosing to do the things they did. No one forced them to rob, kill, rape and mutilate those people. They chose to do those things according to their own free will. They knew the penalty for their crimes before committing them. And when Ranger Hart hangs them, they will have done it to themselves. They were caught, tried by an honest jury and found guilty. I simply applied the law as it is written to the crimes that were committed. They had to know they would eventually get caught. All criminals do, sooner or later. But enough about my work. I would rather focus on you. You are much more pleasant."

"Hmmm," Ruth took a sip of her wine and grinned, "I wonder what Mrs. Stanley would say if she heard you say that?"

"I believe my mother would be both shocked and happy."

"I beg your pardon," Ruth giggled, "but I wasn't referring to your mother, Mr. Stanley."

"I know what you were referring to, but..." he leaned across the table and grinned, "I don't have a wife."

"Really?"

"Really. The only spouse I've ever had is my job. So you are in no danger of breaking up a happy marriage by having dinner with me."

"Well, that is refreshing to know." Ruth heaved a sigh as she visibly relaxed. "I've honestly had enough lies and deception to last a lifetime. I came here tonight expecting you to try to talk me into your hotel room."

Buford paused and fidgeted with his napkin as the Lehmann's cook brought their steaks and baked potatoes to the table.

"Frankly, I am going to try to do that exact thing. But..." he reached across the table and grabbed her wrist as she threw her napkin on the table and tried to get up, "not like you think."

"Oh...I'm sure you have a really good line, Your Honor. Go on...I'd really like to hear it." She sank back into her chair.

"I know you just buried your husband, and this may seem very inappropriate...I would like you to return to San

Antonio with me. Not as my friend or even my mistress. I'm asking you to be my wife."

Ruth stared opened-mouthed before laughing. "Are you serious?"

"I am most definitely serious, Mrs. Rogers. I wouldn't be asking this soon, but I don't have much time. I must leave tomorrow morning for San Antonio. Look," he said as she slowly shook her head, "I know how your husband was treating you, and I also know you didn't love him. Will you marry me, Mrs. Rogers?"

"Mr. Stanley…Your Honor, you hardly know me. We only met three days ago, and you don't know my situation. I haven't been totally honest with you and Ranger Hart. I am not some innocent school girl. As Marshal Best would say, I've been down a few trails and collected a lot of dust. No," she shook her head, "you seem like a decent sort of fellow, and I thank you for your offer, but I couldn't do that to you or your mother."

"Mrs. Rogers," he knelt beside her chair and kissed her hand, "I know all I need to know about you. When I said the only wife I've had is my job, I meant it. I am possibly the loneliest man on the face of this earth. I never knew it until I saw you crossing the street. I honestly envied and hated that man you were with."

"I didn't envy Benjamin, but I certainly grew to hate him," Ruth said with a dry giggle.

"Please, let me finish. It is my turn to be honest with you, and I'm finding this difficult, to say the least."

"I'm sorry." She leaned forward to search his eyes, "but…why me? You are possibly the kindest, gentlest and most generous man in the world. Why would you choose me? You can't possible love me."

"Why would it surprise you that someone would love you?"

"Because no man ever has but Billy Mayfield, and he's dead."

"All I am asking is for you to give me a chance to make you happy, Mrs. Rogers. In a few weeks my father will be retiring, and they've already asked me to take over his courtroom. All my life, I've wanted to be like my father. When I was in college, I focused on my studies and passed my bar exam with ease. I became a judge after practicing law only a few years. I became my father, Mrs. Rogers, but I forgot one important thing. My father took time to fall in love and marry my mother. He goes home to her every evening, while I'll be stuck in San Antonio, in a large house with a housekeeper and a cook, but totally alone. I will have no one to talk to, or to love.

"I can promise I will never treat you the way the others have, Mrs. Rogers. You won't worry about having your face bruised, or being ordered around and yelled at. I will never lie to you or sleep with another woman. I am hard-working and honest. All I am asking is to make you happy."

Ruth stared at him before shaking her head. "I…I just can't marry you."

"And why not? I can promise I'll make you a good husband. I'll love and adore you as long as you live."

"Please, Mr. Stanley…Your Honor…don't make me tell you why. I just…can't marry you."

"Mrs. Rogers, I am not one to beg, but you'll find me a persistent man. Why won't you marry me?"

Ruth covered her mouth as tears ran freely down both cheeks. "Benjamin and I were never married. He promised to marry me and…and take me away from Cool Water. But he kept making excuses and postponing the wedding and now he's dead. We were living in sin."

"Well, I can assure you that won't be a problem with me. I'll marry you tomorrow…even tonight, if you wish. After all, I am a judge," Buford said with a chuckle. "Is there another problem bothering you?"

"Yes, I…I am pretty sure I am going to have his baby. Oh God! How I hate you for making me say that!" She bolted from her chair and into the darkness.

"Is there something wrong with the lady, Your Honor?" Buford looked up to see the maid holding a dessert tray. "Yes, I'm afraid everything is wrong with Mrs. Rogers."

Chapter 23

The citizens of Eagle Pass stopped to stare as the procession of Texas Rangers made their way through town. Their attention gravitated toward the body draped over a saddle, and toward the wounded. They were used to seeing the rangers bring their prisoners and even a body or two into town. Eagle Pass itself had its roots sunk deep into conflict.

During the Mexican War, a company of Texas Mounted Volunteers under the command of Captain John A. Veatch established an observation post on the Rio Grande. It was opposite the mouth of the Mexican Rio Escondido, near an old smuggler's trail. The crossing was known as *El Paso del Aguilar* due to the large number of Mexican eagles living in the wooded grove along the Escondido. Long after the war had ended, and the military site was abandoned, *El Paso del Aguilar* remained a popular crossing for trappers, frontiersmen, and traders. Fort Duncan was established two miles upstream in 1849, and a small settlement sprang up at the crossing below the post. James Campbell arrived from San Antonio and opened a trading post in 1850. He was soon joined by William Leslie Cazneau and his wife, Jane, and the village changed its name from *El Paso del Aguila* to Eagle Pass. Friedrich Groos contracted to haul supplies for the military and brought seventy Mexican families to settle near the fort. A stage line between Eagle Pass and San Antonio was established in 1851, and Our Lady of Refuge Catholic Church was built in 1852.

But while the settlement continued to grow, things weren't always pleasant and Eagle Pass became known for its violence. The village and fort were frequently attacked by Lipan Apache and Comanche Indians. Large coal deposits were discovered on the opposite bank of the Rio Grande. Piedras Negras sprang to life in 1850, and soon became a haven for fugitive slaves. Both banks of the river were infested with outlaws, killers and thieves. In 1855 James H. Callahan made a gallant, but vain, effort to curb some of the violence when he led three companies of volunteers across the river in pursuit of renegade Lipans and Kicakapoos. The Mexican government took exception to the gesture, and Callahan soon found himself in a battle against Mexican forces on the banks of the Escondido. He fell back and set the village of Piedras Negras on fire before crossing back into Eagle Pass.

Following the Civil War, bands of cattle thieves and fugitives led by John King Fisher dominated Eagle Pass. It took the aid of the Texas Rangers and the coming of the railroad in 1884, linking Eagle Pass to Galveston and San Antonio, to eventually establish law and order. Even John Fisher had gone from being an outlaw to a legitimate rancher, and even a lawman. Clay could remember seeing him once, as he strutted down the street dressed in an ornamented Mexican sombrero, a black Mexican jacket embroidered with gold, a crimson sash, and Mexican boots. He carried two silver-plated, ivory-handled revolvers swinging at his hips. The man was proud as a peacock, and had silver bells attached to his spurs to attract attention. The road leading to his ranch even bore a sign stating: "This is King Fisher's road. Take the other." His ranch was reported to be a haven for drifters and criminals. Like most men who try riding both sides of the law however, John Fisher's life came to a quick end as he and his pal Ben Thompson were gunned down inside the Vaudeville Variety Theater in San Antonio on March 11, 1884. Marshall Best happened to be in

San Antonio at the time, and had overseen the shipment of Fisher's body back to his ranch for burial.

The city now had a teeming population of more than 2,000, who wanted nothing more than to go on with their lives and to be left alone. They had just finished building a new courthouse, and were in the process of building an Episcopal Church, which would be the first Protestant church in the area.

The sight of the wounded woman, being held by a large man dressed in black and covered with blood, had set the town a-buzz. A crowd began to gather as the procession of Rangers halted in front of the doctor's residence and dismounted.

~   ~   ~

Doctor Hubert Adams was a crippled old man with arthritic hands. Clay had considered trying to find another doctor, but had no idea if there was another doctor within miles of Eagle Pass. He figured Teresa might not survive being moved even if there was. He had held her in his arms most of the way, switching between Loco and Diablo. Doctor Adams had his wife administer a dose of laudanum to all three patients, then started working immediately on Teresa. He had the wound cleaned and the bleeding stopped in a matter of minutes.

"How's she doing, Doc," Clay asked, as he brushed past on his way to see the rustler.

"You'll have to wait," he said as he leaned over the wounded horse thief. This man's been shot, and Ranger Griffin has a broken collar bone."

"I was just asking…"

"Ranger Atern," the doctor raised his voice, "get this man out of here and let me do my job."

Clay was ushered from the doctor's office and across the street to the nearest café, where he sat staring at a cup of coffee.

"She's gonna be okay, Clay. You'll see." Ira grinned at him over the brim of his mug. "What is she to you, anyway?"

"She's a pain in my neck." Clay glared at him. "I just don't like seeing any woman hurt. That's all."

"Just asking. Don't get all huffed-up on me. The way you were acting, I naturally thought she might be something special."

"Well, she ain't. Although, she did save my life the day I met her. So I guess you can say she might be a little special."

"I reckon she kind of grows on you." Ira grinned and sipped his coffee.

"So does the plague. How's Griffin gonna be?" Clay asked.

"It's a wait and see proposition. He might be out of the corps. It depends on how his shoulder heals."

"He's a good man."

"Yes, he is," Ira said. "I might need your help explaining what you two were doing out there today. General King isn't gonna look too kindly upon a woman getting shot."

"Nope, I don't think so." Clay shook his head. "You just might be Private Aten by tomorrow morning." He looked down and plucked at the front of his shirt. It was covered with Teresa's blood.

"I sure look a sight. You should've said something, Ira. I've got a fresh shirt in my grip."

The two men sat sipping coffee until Ranger Wayne Lindsey came and got them.

~   ~   ~

"Mr. Griffin should heal and be fine in a matter of weeks. You should be able to move him tomorrow. The outlaw will heal in time for you to hang him. It is Mrs. Romero I'm worried about." Doctor Adams paused and sipped his tea.

"I'd like to move that horse thief to the jail this afternoon, if that's possible," Ira said. "He just might try to run off during the night."

"He's your prisoner, you can do what you like."

"Ain't Mrs. Romero's wound a clean one, Doc?" Clay shifted his feet as the doctor glared at him. "I mean, it didn't hit a lung or anything, did it?"

"No, it didn't puncture her lungs, but there are no *clean* or simple wounds, Mr. Best. Every wound brings a risk of trauma and infection. It might also have caused damage we are not aware of until later. To put it bluntly, Mrs. Romero has lost a lot of blood, as the front of your shirt will attest to. She's weak and running a temperature. I would love to say she is going to recover, but I'm not sure. We'll have to wait and see. The next couple of days should tell us more." He took another sip of tea.

"I really don't understand what possessed a group of men, especially Texas Rangers, to have a woman present during a gunfight. All of you should be locked up. And you had better have that shirt laundered. You look as though you were the one wounded."

"Yes sir. May I look in on her?"

"Yes, you may. But she's asleep, and I don't want her disturbed. Just look. By the way," he added as Clay started to open the door to Teresa's room, "I perceive the lady is Catholic, isn't she?"

"I reckon she is. What's that got to do with anything?"

"Nothing, but I like to know these things. Should some complication arise, I'm sure Mrs. Romero would want a priest to administer the last rites before she passes."

Clay nodded and poked his head through the door. Teresa was sleeping soundly, and looked as though she might have been taking an afternoon nap. He left quietly, then checked into the hotel after seeing the horses were properly cared for. He bathed and shaved his whiskers before changing into a fresh shirt and britches. The lady who cleaned the rooms said she knew of a way of getting bloodstains out of shirts, so he gave her his laundry, and asked her to let him know when it was ready. Clay talked the cook at the café into giving him a bucket of scraps to feed Antonio, then thought briefly about getting himself a bite to eat. But his stomach still felt knotted up inside, so he crossed the street to check in on Teresa. She was still sleeping. Clay scooted a chair near her bed and eventually dozed off.

"Mr. Best?"

"Ma'am?" He looked up to see the doctor's wife smiling in the doorway. She laid a hand against his shoulder and spoke softly.

"I'm sure she will be fine."

"Your husband said…"

"My husband is sometimes gruff with people. He has witnessed a lot of violence and misery in this country, especially during the war. He finds it easier to prepare people for the worst, rather than get their hopes up and have them dashed when a patient dies. He's also very angry that you exposed Mrs. Romero to this type of danger."

"I am too. Believe me."

"I'm sure you are, but it's getting late and my husband and I are going to retire for the evening. You are welcome to stay awhile longer, if you wish. I have the lock on the front door set, so all you have to do is make sure the door is closed and latched when you leave."

~   ~   ~

Clay sat quietly watching Teresa breathe. The woman never moved a muscle until she caught her breath and moaned. He leaped from the chair and almost rushed to pound on the door to the back rooms, but Teresa relaxed into more peaceful sleep. His hand against her brow told him she was still running a fever. It was ten o'clock when he leaned close to her ear and talked in a hushed tone, trying not to disturb Ranger Griffin in the adjoining room.

"Now, you listen to me, young lady. I know you ain't used to taking orders from any man, but I didn't bring you this far to have you die on me. You've been nothing but a royal pain most of the time, and it's high time you started earning your keep. It's your doing that got us mixed up in this mess in the first place. I should be back in Carrizo Springs, looking for a hunk of land I can raise cattle on, instead of being stuck out here and getting shot at by a bunch of highbinders.

"In spite of all that, I've kind of gotten used to having you around and jabbering in my ear. I especially like your cooking. You can whip up some mighty fine vittles, even when you ain't got much to work with. We're kind of like saddle pards, and I'd hate to lose you. The thing is, I've gotten kind of fond of you. Some might even say I love you, in an odd sort of way…kind of like the way you love that old dog of yours. So, you knock this nonsense off. You hear? I'll check back on you in the morning."

Chapter 24

Ruth was awakened from a fitful sleep by someone pounding on her door. She fumbled in the darkness to light the lamp, and heard an angry voice yelling at the intruder, but the pounding continued.

"Just a minute, please." Ruth grabbed her robe. She pulled back the curtain to peek at the predawn blackness outside her window. Tying the sash snugly around her waist, she unlocked the door and opened it slightly, only to have it pushed wide open as Buford Stanley entered.

"Judge Stanley…!"

"I'm sorry, Mrs. Rogers," Terry Connors said. "I tried to stop him, but he wouldn't listen, and he is a judge and…"

"It's alright, Mr. Connors. I will handle this."

A heavyset woman poked her head into the hall and yelled. "Will y'all pipe down? I'm trying to get some sleep!"

"I'm sorry, ma'am. I'll make him stop." Ruth shut her door quietly and turned to glare at Buford. The man had opened her wardrobe and was tossing her clothing onto the bed.

"And what in the world do you think you're doing? Put those things back right now!"

"Where is your luggage? Ah, here we are," he grabbed two large carpet bags from under the bed and opened them. "Would you like to do the packing, or shall I?"

"I'd like for you to get the hell out of my room."

"Oh, that is not very ladylike," he said with a grin. "You'll upset my mother if she hears you using profanity."

"She's liable to hear me use profanity all the way in San Antonio if you don't get out of here this instant. I don't know what you think you're doing, and I don't care if you are a judge. I don't care if you're the president. You can't come into someone's room and start rummaging through their things."

"How right you are, my darling." He smiled and touched the tip of her nose with his finger. She swatted at his hand and received a laugh for her efforts.

"Will you please tell me what you think you are doing?"

"Certainly." He began folding her dresses and placing them in the largest bag. "I am taking you to San Antonio. We can either get married on the way, or wait and have a large wedding once we arrive. I must warn you though, my mother will want to plan the whole thing. She means well, but she tends to take charge when given the chance. It's just her nature."

"Your Honor…Judge Stanley, I'm begging you. I've already turned you down once. What is it going to take to make you understand? I can't marry you. You're a judge, and I'm a tainted lady. I have done things. I was living in sin when you saw me that day. I am not the type of woman you should be choosing for a wife."

He paused with a blue dress in his hand and laughed. "Perhaps you can tell me, Mrs. Rogers, what type of woman should I choose?"

"Certainly not me." She sat on the edge of the bed and folded her hands in her lap.

"Would you cheat on me if we were married?"

"No." She shook her head.

"Would you mistreat our children, or treat my parents with disrespect?"

"No, but…"

"Ah," he held up a finger, "I am the one asking the questions. The facts are, Mrs. Rogers, you wouldn't have to worry about the house. I have a very competent housekeeper. She's also a really good cook, so you wouldn't have to bother with that either. The worst you would have to put up with is my working late occasionally. My father will want to parade you around, bragging about his beautiful-daughter-in-law. He'll also spoil our children rotten."

"That would be fine, except I haven't agreed to marry you, Mister Stanley." Ruth grabbed several dresses from her carpetbag, only to have Buford snatch them from her and stuff them back in.

"Mr. Stanley, why do you keep insisting…? Why won't you please leave me alone?"

"Because," he forced her to sit on the edge of the bed and held her hands, "I am an only child who is used to getting his own way. I've listened to every word you said…all the reasons why we can't get married. Does your past bother me? Certainly. But only because I am jealous that that piece of human debris knew you first, and treated you the way he did. I also know you don't love me right now." He let go of her hands and turned away to grab several petticoats from the wardrobe.

"I am, after all, a judge, and, like a good judge, I weighed all the evidence against our relationship. After deliberating all night on this case, I came to the only logical solution. I would be miserable without you. I am sentencing you to a life of being loved and adored. Do you think you could live with that, Mrs. Rogers?"

"I could certainly live with that, Mr. Stanley. To be honest, I am more fond of you than I've allow myself to let on. But there is someone else to consider. I am fairly certain I am going to have a baby. How would you feel about being father to another man's child?"

He chuckled as he knelt in front of her and kissed her fingers.

"Mrs. Rogers. I haven't been totally honest with you either. My parents could not have children of their own. I lived the first eight years of my life in an orphanage.

Benjamin Rogers may have sired our baby, but I will have the privilege and honor of being his father. The secret will be ours alone. Our son or daughter will never know any different.

"Now," he grabbed another dress, "shall we finish packing?"

Chapter 25

Clay staggered out of bed at the crack of dawn, dressed and drank a cup of coffee in the café. He bumped into Wayne on his way through the door, almost knocking him down.

"Hey, Clay, how are you this morning? I was just fixin' to grab breakfast. Come back and keep me company. I'll buy you another coffee."

"Later, Wayne. I'm gonna check on Mrs. Romero."

"Oh, sure. Tell her I said hi."

The smoke rolling from the chimney at the back of the doctor's office told Clay that Mrs. Adams was up and about, and was more than likely fixing the cantankerous old doctor breakfast. Clay opened the front door and froze in his tracks. The door to Teresa's room was standing open, and a priest was hovering over the bed, praying. The doctor was bent over Teresa on the opposite side, with his wife crowded closely by.

"Aw, Lordy!" Clay moaned as he slumped against the door post. Mrs. Adams rushed toward him with a warm smile and grabbed his arm.

"There you are. I was wondering when you might get here. I heard you leave last night, and knew you would be tired." She gave his arm a tug. "Come on, she's been asking about you."

"Huh?" He cocked his head to one side.

"Mrs. Romero's woke up awhile ago, and she's been asking for you."

Clay stood at the foot of the bed staring, as the doctor spooned oatmeal into Teresa's mouth. The woman swallowed, and smiled at him before speaking in a raspy voice.

"*Buenos dias, Señor* Best. How are you?"

"I reckon I'm doing just fine. But I ought to turn you over my knee and beat the daylights out of you. You liked to scared the dickens out of me. I come in here and seen this padre praying. I thought you were done for, and he was giving you the last rites."

The priest burst out laughing. "No, I am sorry. *Señor* Best, is it? I am Father Francisco." He shook Clay's hand. "I heard only this morning that a young Mexican woman had been wounded, and I came to see how she was doing. I see she is doing much better than I was told, so I was giving her a simple blessing. I think she is anxious to visit with you, so I will leave you two alone."

"Yeah, thanks, Padre."

"Here, you should be doing this." Doctor Adams shoved the bowl of oatmeal toward Clay. "I haven't eaten my breakfast, and I need to check on the other wounded folk you brought in." His wife smiled, patted Clay on the arm, and followed her husband through the door.

"Well, I reckon it's just you and me." Clay sat in the chair and grabbed the spoon. "You need to listen to me once in awhile. I hollered for you to stop, but you just kept right on going and got yourself shot."

"*Si*, you were right, *Señor* Best," she said with a nod, then closed her eyes and winced. "It still hurts sometimes."

"I reckon it's gonna do that until it gets fully healed. Let that be a reminder for you to listen."

"*Si*, I will listen from now on."

"Good."

She finished her oatmeal and Clay held a mug of lukewarm coffee for her to drink. He dabbed her lips with a napkin and grinned.

"Well, I reckon I ought to go eat something myself. I ain't really ett since noon yesterday. Feeding you breakfast reminded me I'm near starving to death."

He rose to his feet and gave her a crooked grin. "I'm glad you're feeling better."

"*Señor* Best?" she said as he started to leave.

"Ma'am?"

"I love you too."

"P-pardon?" He turned slowly and approached the bed.

"You said last night you love me, and I say I love you too."

"I never said…" He paused as he remembered leaning close to her ear and what he had said. He snickered and shoved his hands deep inside his pockets.

"Yeah, I reckon I did say it, didn't I?"

"*Si,*" she said with a nod.

"Okay, I'll be back, so don't go nowhere."

Chapter 26

Captain Jones of the Texas Rangers gave Ira a swift verbal kick in the rear for allowing Teresa to be present when they encountered the horse thieves. Then he gave Clay a good cussing Texas style, in which he called him every lowdown critter under the sun. Both men took their reprimands in good graces, and promised to never let it happen again. Ira said he figured they'd gotten off easy, then left for Lampasas County to settle a rash of wire-cutting.

Clay got his laundry back with Teresa's blood still visible on the shirt.

"I'm sorry, Mr. Best. I can usually get stains like that out, but this one had set too long." He paid the lady anyway, deciding to keep the shirt as a reminder never to do something that stupid again.

He spent most of the afternoon taking short walks around the doctor's residence with Teresa. His relationship with June had been a quiet, relaxing one, for neither of them were talkers by nature. Teresa was different though, and he decided that the man who married Teresa Romero would have to be deaf or he would never have a moment's peace. She had said very little after getting shot. Now it was as though a river of words had gotten dammed up inside her throat, and wanted to get out. He pulled his boots off that evening and fell asleep in the hotel, with her voice ringing in his ears. It was still preferable to seeing her lying in the bed near death.

~   ~   ~

Teresa was on her feet the fourth morning, acting like her old self. The doctor accosted Clay as he came through the door.

"I guess I owe you some sort of apology, Mr. Best. This woman won't obey my orders, and won't stay out of the little hair I have left. She keeps trying to tell me how to do my job. I would appreciate it if you would take her somewhere and let her get shot. But please, don't bring her back here when she does." He glared at Teresa before leaving the room.

"She's going to be fine," Mrs. Adams said quietly, giving Clay's arm a gentle squeeze. "She's ready to leave. Just take it easy, and make sure she keeps her arm in the sling. Keep the wound clean and dry. Then have a doctor remove the stitches in about two weeks. After that, she should be as good as new."

"Thank you, ma'am. What do we owe you?" Clay dug his billfold out of his pocket.

"The bill has already been paid by the Texas Rangers. Just be careful looking for whoever it is you are looking for. We'd hate to see you back here again, unless it's to say hello," she said with a laugh.

"What'd you do to that old man to get him so mad at you?" Clay asked as they crossed the dusty street.

"He is a horse-doctor who will not listen to anyone but himself," she said angrily. "A woman brings in a little *niño* who is coughing, and I tell him how my grandmother makes a cough better with charanda and lime. But would he listen? No, he is a stubborn burro."

Clay laughed as he held the door of the café open. He was familiar with the Indian liquor made from a mixture of fermenting agave sap and sugar cane. He had gotten a headache from drinking charanda more than once. "Well, I never thought about using it that way, but I reckon it might cure a cough. Either that, or kill you."

Conversation inside the small café ceased and heads turned as they entered. Several cowboys pushed back from a table and argued over who got to hold Teresa's chair.

"*Gracias caballeros.*" Teresa flashed them a warm smile as she seated herself. "You are very kind."

"Oh, no problem, ma'am. If you need anything while you're in town, just ask for Rio and I'll see that you get it."

"*Gracias Señor* Rio."

"They are nice boys, don't you think, *Señor* Best?" she said as the cowboys moved to the counter. Clay grinned as they cast admiring glances toward Teresa's back.

News always traveled fast in small towns. Any news, no matter how big or small, became the topic of discussion for days. However, problems arose when newspapers expanded the actual events with rumors and speculation, and in some cases outright fiction, in order to sell papers. The local paper had run a front page article the previous day, claiming Teresa Romero was actually an agent working with the Texas Rangers. According to the story, her job was to infiltrate bandit gangs and woo their leaders with her wiles and beauty, then pass important information to the rangers. According to the paper, her true identity had been discovered, and the rangers, with the aid of Marshal Clay Best, had to charge the gang of rustlers with guns blazing in order to rescue their spy. It didn't matter that the entire story had been concocted by the author's imagination and aided with a bottle of bourbon. People who had read the story believed it.

"Yeah, I reckon they are pretty nice at that. But you are mighty good to look at, and it doesn't hurt to be the most popular woman in South Texas either."

"*¿Qué?* What are you saying, *Señor* Best? Why should people care who Teresa Romero is?"

Clay chuckled, then ordered plates of steak, fried potatoes, biscuits and gravy with a pot of coffee before relaying the contents of the front page article.

"But…that is not true! Why would he say such things?"

"To sell newspapers, would be my guess." Clay took a sip of coffee and grinned at her.

"Where is this man who wrote these lies? What are we going to do about…such…" She shook her head and waved her hand in frustration.

"We're gonna sit right here and enjoy our dinner. Then I'm taking you to the hotel. I've already got you a room and moved your things in there. Then we're going to follow that doctor's orders and take it easy for the next few days until you get some of your strength back. That's what we're gonna do," he said with a nod.

"But what about what the newspaper is saying?"

"What about it? It doesn't matter what a few folks around here think, and they'll forget about you soon enough once the next story gets printed. You might as well enjoy being popular while you can." A quick glance around the café told Clay what the residents of Eagle Pass actually thought of the woman seated across the table. Not one person had left the café since they arrived, including Rio and his friends, who were still at the counter. Several patrons were sitting with empty plates, watching and waiting to hear what either of them might say.

"So, as I was saying, I reckon once you're up to snuff, we'll pack our grip and mosey down the road," Clay said as the waitress brought their food. Teresa grabbed the fork in her left hand and stared at the gravy-smothered steak on her plate.

"Here, let me give you a hand," Clay said as he cut the meal into bite-sized pieces. "I reckon you might've been able to gnaw it off the bone, but it wouldn't look too ladylike."

"*Gracias*. So, where do we go next, *Señor* Best?" she asked as Clay finished cutting her meat. "What is the name?"

she mumbled to herself. "Did not Ranger Wayne say he saw the *señorita*, at someone's rancho?"

"I reckon he did at that. The Lehmann Ranch, but we're not going there," Clay said as he cut a hunk of his own steak and shoved it in his mouth.

"*¿Qué?* Where are we going?"

"I'm taking you back to Carrizo Springs. Then I reckon I'll mosey back up here and fetch Ruth home, if she's still anywheres around."

Teresa glared at him across the table before slamming her palm against the table. "No, *Señor* Best! I will go to the rancho and find the *señorita* with you!"

"No you ain't." Clay shook his head and stared at his plate as he chewed. Teresa muttered several more words in Spanish that he vaguely recognized as curses, before leaping to her feet.

"*Señors*," she said loudly. "This man, *Señor* Clay Best, is a big liar." She gestured toward him as if she were presenting a dignitary. "He promises to take me to find *Señorita* Ruth Bishop and share in the reward her grandfather offers. But now he says I am not welcome. He also says he loves me. I go with him, cook his meals and wash his clothes and spend many nights alone with him. But now he says I must return to my casa in Carrizo Springs, because he doesn't want me anymore. So, what do you think? I say he is a liar."

Clay swallowed as every man inside the café stood to his feet.

"He's worse than that, ma'am. Want us to take him outside and teach him some manners?" Rio asked as he unbuckled his gun belt. Clay glanced around the room, figuring he might be able to handle two or three of them by himself, but he certainly couldn't handle every man in the café. He laid his fork on the table and raised both hands in surrender.

"Mind if I say my piece before you boys bust me to smithereens?"

"Better talk fast," growled a big man at the next table as he removed his hat.

"It ain't that anything she said isn't true, but the reason I want her to go home is, I just don't want to see her hurt again. None of you held her in your arms after that rustler shot her, or saw her lying in that bed across the street, near death. I did, and it about ripped my insides out. I lost my wife awhile back, and I thought I'd lost this woman for sure. We might only be friends at this point, but I don't ever want to go through that again. I honestly thought I was done for."

"Well, that throws a different loop on things," Rio said. "What do you think, ma'am? Figure he's telling it like it is?"

Teresa stared at him with watery eyes and sat back down.

"*Bueno, gracias.*" She took a bite of steak and chewed vigorously as the men returned to their seats.

"Thanks. Now, can we finish eating in peace, or should I keep my pistol handy?"

"We finish eating," she said with a nod. "But," she paused with another bite halfway to her mouth and pointed her fork at him, "we finish talking later. *¿Bueno?*"

"Yes, ma'am. We'll talk."

Chapter 27

The Lehmann Ranch was a small settlement approximately fifteen miles north of Eagle Pass, lying on the banks of the Rio Grande. The residents were mostly Mexican ranch employees and their families. They could however, boast of having their very own post office with Frank R. Lehmann as postmaster. They also had two stores and a one-teacher school with thirty-eight students. The only drinking establishment was a makeshift tent with three open sides that could quickly be covered with canvas during bad weather. The bar itself was constructed by laying several planks on top of empty barrels. Two small tables were flanked by empty crates and barrels for the customers to sit on. A hand-painted sign called the establishment Lucky Seven.

Clay set a leisurely pace, mainly to see how Teresa would hold up physically in the heat on horseback. It was late afternoon when they rode into the settlement to find it bustling with people. They dismounted, and were worming their way toward one of the stores, when a drunken cowboy stumbled out of the Lucky Seven and almost knocked Teresa down.

"Eeeyah! Howdy, pretty lady. Care for a dance?"

Teresa gave him a shove as two equally drunken men came to the front of the tent and laughed.

"No? Well, how about a drink?" He held up a bottle as Antonio lunged at him with a loud bark. He staggered backward and Clay clubbed him on the head.

"Hey, there weren't no need for that," one of the men protested. "He was just having a little fun."

"I reckon you're right. I could've let this dog kill him. You try offending Miss Romero like your friend was doing, and see what happens." Clay tied the horses to the hitching rail and took Teresa's arm. He paused to glare at the men. "Antonio," he said to the dog, "keep an eye on our grip." The dog emitted a low rumble from his chest as he obediently took a position between the men and the hitching rail.

Clay held tightly to Teresa, slipping through the crowd and inside the store. They wormed their way past several customers toward the counter. "May I help you?" asked a haggard-looking man with a receding hairline as they approached.

"I'm Clay Best and this young woman is Teresa Romero from Carrizo Springs. We just came into town and didn't see any hotel. Miss Romero is feeling poorly, and we were wondering, is there a place we can bunk for the night?"

"Clay Best. I've heard of you. As far as finding a place to stay, the answer's both yes and no. There is a boarding house of sorts just north of town, but you won't find any rooms available. As you can tell, everyone for miles around is here for the hanging."

"Hanging? What hanging?" Clay cast a glance toward Teresa as she gasped.

"Why, they are hanging the Walker brothers tomorrow at noon right down there near the river. The Texas Rangers caught 'em about two weeks ago and brought 'em in. They've been tried and found guilty. Ranger Hart is going to do the honors himself. Everyone is glad to be rid of 'em, so they're celebrating early."

"What do these men do to get hanged?" Teresa asked.

"What did they do? You must have really been out of touch, miss. I thought folks in Carrizo Springs would know about the Walkers. I've got a picture of them right here." He dug a wanted poster from under the counter and held it proudly. The two men depicted in the artist's drawing were bearded, hard-looking men with long hair and evil eyes. Teresa stared at the poster as the storekeeper continued.

"The Walker brothers came down from Arkansas through the Indian Territory and into Texas, robbing and burning small farms and ranches along the way. They supposedly killed several travelers to boot. But the main reason they're getting hung so quickly is," he leaned across the counter and talked in a hushed tone as two women entered the store, "they raped several women while they were at it. They seemed to like young girls, although I heard it said during the trial they molested one grandmother. The one that really got folks riled was when they molested and killed Louise Carlson just five miles north of here. The Carlson's were nice, peaceful folks who had a small farm. Louise was a pretty little thing, only eight years old. The rangers come up on them right after they'd finished killing her, and saw 'em leaving the farm. They made a chase out of it, but Ranger Hart caught 'em trying to make it across the river. The idiots didn't know where to cross and got bogged down in some mud. I say it's good riddance to 'em both, and I'm gonna have Ranger Hart sign this poster when he's finished hanging the sons-of-bitches."

"*Madre de Dios*," Teresa said, crossing herself.

"Well, much obliged." Clay took Teresa's arm. "I was hoping there might be someplace Miss Romero might rest, but I reckon we'll just mosey down the road."

"You might check with George Higgins, down at the livery. His wife runs the café next door." He motioned with his head. "I hear tell he has a small room over the stalls he uses when Edith's relatives come to visit. It ain't much, but he may be willing to rent it to you folks. Tell him Hank sent you."

"Much obliged," Clay said with a nod. Clay eyed the three cowboys as he untied their horses. The one he had clubbed was sitting on the ground, holding a hand to his wounded head. Antonio was still obediently standing guard between the men and the hitching rail.

"Y'all can move now. Just remember your manners around Miss Romero. I wasn't around to save the last idgit who grabbed hold of her, and Antonio ate him."

"Ate him?" one of the men almost shouted.

"Yes sir, we'll mind our manners," a second man said.

"Why did you tell those men that?" Teresa asked as they walked toward the livery. "Antonio doesn't eat people, he bites them."

"What do you care? The word will spread and I won't have to be looking out for you while we're in town."

Chapter 28

George Higgins rented out the room above the stables for a dollar a day. Hot water for a bath was another dollar if they carried it themselves, and the horses were fifty cents each. Clay grumbled as he gave the owner three dollars and fifty cents. He unpacked their horses and Teresa led the way up a set of creaky stairs. Clay dumped their grip in a corner. The room was small, with a single bed sporting a thin mattress. A wooden chair that seemed to have one short leg sat in the corner. A mirror with a crack running through the middle hung on the wall opposite the bed.

"Well, nothing but the best," Clay said with a laugh. "I guess we'd better see about that bath, and have a look at your shoulder."

George had water heating in a galvanized washtub over a fire in the yard. Clay carried several bucketfuls to a lean-to attached to the back of the stables. The small room did contain a galvanized bathtub, but the lean-to itself only had three walls, with the open side facing away from the stable. Teresa bathed first as Clay stationed himself at the opening to discourage any curious lookers. After she had dressed, Clay took his turn in the same water. He carried a bucketful of fresh water to their room for shaving and washing in the morning.

"Okay, let me have a look-see at your shoulder."

"*Bien.*" Teresa unbuttoned her blouse and pulled it off her right shoulder, before reaching behind her head with her left hand to pull her long hair back. Clay had to struggle to keep his eyes from drifting toward the cleavage between her breasts as he gently pulled the bandage from the smooth, copper skin.

"Mmm, looks like its healing just fine. You're gonna have a nice scar, thanks to that thieving highbinder," he said as he applied sulfur powder to a fresh bandage.

"You killed that man after he shot me, didn't you?"

"I reckon I did. Why?"

"Then we are even. I killed the man who pointed a gun at you, and you killed the man who shot me when I wouldn't listen. We are now, how do you say…?"

"Saddle-pards?"

"*Si*, saddle-pards. We saved each other, so we become saddle-pards."

"Huh, I reckon we are even. Except you killed Donaldson before he plugged me, and I waited until you got shot, so I still owe you. There." He pulled her blouse back over her shoulder. "You can button yourself up. I ain't no doctor, but I'd say you're doing fine."

"*Gracias*." She gave him an impish grin. "You are a nice man, *Señor* Best, in here." She patted his chest and turned away to button her blouse.

~   ~   ~

The café was small but clean, and the aroma as they entered made Clay's mouth water.

"Sit yourselves anywhere you want. Folks won't start coming in for another half-hour or so. My name's Edith Higgins. Where y'all from?" She was a large-boned woman dressed in a blue cotton dress with perspiration stains under each arm. Edith adjusted the soiled white apron around her waist as she approached their table. Her blond hair was streaked with gray and pulled tightly in a bun, with a wayward strand clinging to her left cheek. Clay nodded his approval. She was true Texan and more than the equal of her husband.

"Mrs. Romero's from Carrrizo Springs. I hail from Cool Water myself."

"Cool Water?" She gave a snort as she poured the coffee. "Now that's a place to be shed of. Y'all here for the hanging?"

"No, just passing through. You know Cool Water?"

"Yeah, we spent the best part of two months there a few years back. George and me worked for Les Bishop 'till we got smart. George figured he'd best be getting me away before I killed that old bastard, so we come here. Can't say I'm sorry either. I don't remember seeing you there."

"I spent the past year and a half as marshal of Cool Water. It took my wife dying before I got smart."

"Sorry to hear that. What can I get you folks?"

"Just whatever you figure is the best."

"You've got it. I've got two of the prettiest steaks you've ever laid eyes on, just waiting to be eaten." She rounded the counter and tossed the steaks into a frying pan.

"You were lucky to find a room. I didn't believe there were any left."

"We didn't. We're renting that room your husband's got above the stables."

"That right?" Edith leaned against the counter and gave a crooked grin. "I'll bet that old tightwad is charging you plenty, ain't he? I think some of Les Bishop's charm rubbed off on him. I'll have a talk with George tonight."

Clay and Teresa sipped their coffee and discussed their plans until Edith slid plates piled high with steaks, fried potatoes and biscuits in front of them. Then she brought two large slices of apple pie as people began pouring through the door. Clay was washing his pie down with another cup of coffee when a tall young man entered, stopping near their table.

"Could I get a cup of coffee, Edith?"

"Sure thing, Curt. Why don't you introduce yourself to Clay Best and Teresa Romero?"

"That's exactly what I plan to do." He gave Clay a grin as he pulled an empty chair to their table. He was sporting a silver star on his vest. "Mind if I sit with you folks awhile? Name's Curtis Hart. Some folks call us rangers the law around these parts, what little there is."

"Suit yourself, seeing as you're already seated. What can we do for you?"

"Nothing much," he said with a snicker. "There's a nasty rumor going around that that dog lying outside the door eats people. Wanna tell me about that?"

"An *hombre* grabbed me today, and *Señor* Best tells him that to make him leave me alone. But Antonio never eats people," Teresa said, shaking her head. "He bites them when they bother me."

"I figured as much. And I suppose that's one of the reasons you gave Mississippi that lump on his head?"

"Was that his handle? All I know is he was being untoward to this lady. I just learned him some manners."

"He needed some. I'd of probably done worse. Y'all here for the hanging?"

"No, we're looking for someone." Clay pulled Ruth's picture from his vest and passed it across the table. "Her name's Ruth Bishop. Her grandpa got a ransom note saying she'd been kidnapped, but I figure she just run off. We heard from one of the rangers she might be here. You know anything about her?"

"Yeah, sure do," Curt nodded, "she was here with a big shakes of a fellow, who really thought he was something. They wandered in here a few weeks back and took a room at the boarding house. Folks around here didn't like him much, but she seemed nice enough."

"Know where they are now?" Clay sipped his coffee.

"Sure, at least I know where he is. I can take you to him. He's right out there in the cemetery. And, I've got a pretty good idea where the girl is. She left a few days after her boyfriend got hisself killed."

"Killed? How'd it happen?" Clay refilled their cups from the pot on the table.

"Well, I was out looking for the Walker brothers myself. I only pass through here every once in awhile and spend a day or two. Lehmann Ranch is normally a pretty quiet place. I might not know all the particulars, but I can tell you what I know." He shrugged and sipped his coffee. "A couple of new fellers drifted in here. Folks said they were nice and quiet...older men. They made themselves at home in the Lucky Seven, playing faro mostly for fun. You know...penny-ante stuff. Some folks figured they might've known the dealer from way back somewhere. Anyway, the big man horned into their game, and kept upping the ante. Pretty soon the game got serious and he lost all his money. He left, but came back later with another poke and lost that one too. Terry at the boardinghouse figured it might've been this girl's money he was losing.

"Anyway, the numbskull jumped up accusing the men of cheating and went for a gun. One of the new fellers was a whole lot quicker, and gutted him with a knife before he could clear leather. The two drifters were long-gone when I got back to the ranch. Someone said the one who did the killing called himself Kiowa Johnson."

"Kiowa? The other feller wasn't Baldy Russell, was he?" Clay asked.

"I can't say I know," Curt said with a shrug. "The last I heard of Russell, he was hiding out somewhere in Arizona. He may be back, but I ain't heard anything if he is. This girl," he held Ruth's picture up, "left about a week ago with a real nice man who took a liking to her. They were talking about getting married, and she could do worse."

"Know where they might be?" Clay asked as the ranger downed the last of his coffee and stood.

. "Sure do." He passed Ruth's picture back to Clay. "She sold the team and buggy to Frank Lehmann to pay her bill at the boarding house. It was a pretty nice rig, too. I wouldn't have minded having the horses myself, but I wouldn't have any use for a buggy. Anyway, after settling her debts with Terry, she climbed on the train with Buford Stanley, headed toward San Antonio. Buford's the new circuit judge Governor Ireland appointed awhile back."

"*Carumba*," Teresa said, shaking her head. "It did not take the *señorita* long to find another man, did it?"

"Well, I gather from what folks say, it was long over between her and Rogers before he got hisself kilt. She was sporting some bruises when I saw her, and Terry said Rogers had just beaten the hell out of her a couple of hours before Kiowa did for him. I didn't see her shed many tears when we put him down. She was alone, and didn't know anyone or have any money." He cocked his head to one side. "Judge Stanley's a nice-looking feller who smells nice and has money. I wouldn't be too hard on her."

"Much obliged." Clay shook the ranger's hand and paid their bill.

"Think nothing of it. What are you going to do when you find her?"

"It depends on her situation. If she's happy, I'll give her grandpa's regards. If not, take her home," Clay said with a shrug.

Chapter 29

Clay stood outside the door while Teresa got ready for bed, then spread his bedroll on the floor and removed his boots. "Yah!" he yelled and threw one of the boots as a mouse scampered across the floor. "Get out of here, you thieving varmint."

"*Señor* Best, why do you sleep on the floor?"

He turned to stare at her. She was propped on one elbow and grinning at him.

"I do not take much room, *señor*. You may sleep here, if you wish." She patted the mattress.

"No, I'll do just fine, but thanks anyway. Maybe you could turn the other way while I get undressed?"

"*Señor*, you may not know this, but I see you many times in your, how do you say…long-johns. Your underthings you sleep in cover you well."

"Maybe so, but turn you head just the same."

"*Si*, as you wish."

She rolled to face the wall and Clay stripped to his long-johns. He slipped between the blankets before telling her it was okay to turn around.

"*Señor* Best?"

"What now?"

"There are *ratones* in this place. Throwing your boot will not make them go away. You had better sleep here with me. I will not bite you, but they will."

"I reckon you're right, ma'am." He shook his head. "As tempting as that offer is, I'd better not. I don't believe a man should sleep with a woman he ain't married to. Besides, I don't think that rickety thing would hold the both of us. You'd better take the bed, and I'll bunk here."

"As you wish. *Buenas noches, Señor* Best."

"Good night, ma'am."

~   ~   ~

Clay woke with a stiff neck. The sun was beginning to turn the eastern sky pink outside the single dusty window in the loft. He grabbed for the blanket, intending to toss it back, and grabbed an extra arm instead. Teresa gave a soft moan as she snuggled closer against his back.

"Good God! Ma'am?"

He could feel her warm breath against the back of his neck as she slept.

"Ma'am?" He tugged against her arm.

"Mmmm, *buenos días, Señor* Best." She drew him closer with the arm draped across his chest.

"Ma'am, what are you doing on the floor? I thought you had the bed."

"*Sí*, but I have bad dreams. Those men…the ones in the picture? They come in my dreams and do the things to me that they do to the grandmother and little *niña*. I was frightened and come close to you so I can sleep. I am sorry to bother you, *Señor* Best."

"Oddly enough, you didn't bother me. That's what's got me worried. Someone might've slipped in here and I wouldn't have noticed. Do you get nightmares often?"

"*¿Qué?*"

"Nightmares…bad dreams? How often do you get them?"

"Mmmm," she rolled to her back and locked her arm in his, tangling her fingers with his, "sometimes. They came every night at first, but now they come just sometimes. I do not remember when my mother and papa died. I was just a little *niña*, and my grandmother and grandpapa took care of me. Then grandpapa died, and it hurts bad. Then I meet Refugio, and he makes things better. He holds me in the night and I am safe, but he died when the Comanche came, and I feel hurt inside and I am afraid. I still have my grandmother, but she is old and sick, and cannot talk or feed herself.

"I try to make friends with the man from the *cantina*, but he comes and does the same things to me that those men in the picture did, but he does not kill me. I would have liked it better if he had killed me, *señor*. Then he tells others and they come to do the same things, but I chase them away with Refugio's pistol, and Miguel gives me Antonio to chase the men away.

"Then Rob comes to stay at my *casa*. He is young, but he is big and strong, and treats me nice…like you. The men stop coming and I feel safe once more, and the bad dreams do not come in the middle of the night. But his brother takes him away, and they do not come back. And my grandmother dies and I am alone." She rolled to stare into his face. Her hair was a mass of tangled black curls framing her face, and her eyes were dark pools glistening in the early morning light.

"Do you know what it means to be alone, *Señor* Best? When you have no one to love or care about you…to chase the bad dreams away?"

"Yes, ma'am, I reckon I do."

"That is why I sleep with you last night. Is it okay?"

"Yes ma'am, I reckon it is."

"*Gracias Señor* Clay." She kissed his hand and sat up.

Clay pulled on his pants and boots and crammed his hat on his head. He draped the gunbelt across his shoulder and almost ran to the outhouse, wondering why women chose to carry on with long conversations first thing in the morning. She could've said the same thing over a hot cup of coffee and a plate of flapjacks, after he'd visited the privy.

~   ~   ~

"I thought you did not care to watch this."

"I don't, but I think you need to." The leather creaked as Clay shifted in his saddle. They were on horseback standing at the edge of the crowd, as the wagon carrying Ned and Layton Walker made its way toward the river. The men were handcuffed to a metal ring in the bed, while a guard armed with a shotgun kept watch. Ranger Curtis Hart was seated next to George Higgins. George stopped the wagon under a makeshift gallows with two ropes draped over the beam, and Ranger Hart climbed into the bed as George held the team steady. The guard readied the shotgun as the sheriff unlocked the chain.

"Alright boys, time to stand." He grabbed the prisoners by the arm and gave a tug.

"Get you filthy hands off me!" Layton yelled, and pulled back.

"We can do this the hard way if that's what you want." The ranger gave a nod and three husky men leaped into the wagon and grabbed Layton Walker, forcing him to stand. His brother rose to his feet with minimal effort, and stood beside his brother looking dazed.

"Y'all have any last words?"

Ned shook his head as Layton sneered.

"Yeah, go to hell!"

"No, thanks," Ranger Hart said as he slipped a gunnysack over each head. "I've already saddled my bronc next to Jesus, and figure I wouldn't like hell one bit, especially with you two being there." He slipped a noose over each head and snugged them. The three men in the wagon leaped to the ground just as Ranger Hart gripped the back of the seat and patted George on the shoulder. The big man gave the reins a shake and the wagon rolled forward, leaving Ned and Layton Walker suspended in mid air.

"*Madre de Dios*, have mercy on their souls," Teresa said, gripping the crucifix draped around her neck.

"Let's go," Clay said, nudging Loco forward. He touched the brim of his hat and gave the ranger a nod as they passed the wagon. They were approximately a mile out of town when Teresa trotted Diablo close.

"Why did you make me watch, *Señor* Best? I did not care for it at all."

"I wanted you to see, so you'd know those two varmints are dead. They won't be hurting folks anymore." He reached for her gloved hand and gave it a gentle squeeze.

"They're gone, Teresa. They won't be bothering your dreams anymore."

Chapter 30

They rode eastward from Lehmann Ranch toward the Anacacho Mountains. Teresa insisted she felt fine, but Clay had a suspicion that she had not yet regained her full strength. He set a leisurely pace, resting often, but by mid afternoon she had begun to sag in the saddle.

He pulled Loco next to Diablo and patted Teresa's shoulder. "Think you can hang on for a couple more miles? It's been awhile since I've been this way, but if I remember correctly, there's a trading post right up ahead."

"I am fine, *Señor* Best."

"No, you're not. Let me know if we need to stop before we reach the trading post."

"*Bien.*" She nodded.

The sun beat down on their backs as they walked their horses. Teresa almost fell, so Clay took hold of her arm as the trading post came into sight.

"See? There it is, about a quarter-mile up the road. Think you can make it that far?"

"*Si,*" she said, straightening herself in the saddle. Clay let go of her arm. He guided their tired mounts toward the hitching rail and helped her dismount.

"Come on, let's get you inside. I'll water the horses later." He guided her through the door and toward a cane-back chair near a table.

"Get her out of here!"

As Clay jerked around, he saw a burly man serving drinks to a couple of dusty cowboys leaning against a crude bar. His eyes darted quickly around the room to find it empty except for the men at the bar and one man seated in a chair in the opposite corner.

"Huh?"

"You heard me. Her kind ain't welcome here. This is a whites-only establishment." The surly man rounded the corner of the bar and grabbed an ax handle from a barrel as he crossed the room.

"Well, I reckon that might be true. But this woman's sick, and needs to get inside out of the sun."

"I don't give a damn if she's dying." He raised the ax handle. "Get your Mexican whore and get outta…" He froze as Clay whipped his pistol from his holster and cocked the hammer.

"I ought to blow your head off and burn this place to the ground." The man backed away as Clay came toward him. The two men at the bar laughed and downed their drinks.

"Looks like you bit off more'n you can chew, Luke," one of them said as he refilled their glasses.

"Now, you're gonna get the lady a cup of cool water and let her sit a minute. Then we'll gladly leave. Understand?"

"*Señor*," Teresa said, tugging on Clay's arm. "Come, we go."

"Not until you get a drink of water and rest."

"I shall drink from the canteen. This man does not want us here. Come." She tugged harder on his sleeve.

Clay took the ax handle from the bartender's hand and tossed it across the room.

"You're getting off easy, mister. If it was up to me, I'd take your head off and feed it to you, one piece at a time." He took Teresa's hand and backed toward the door.

"You and your Mexican whore just keep away from here," the barkeep yelled as they reached the door.

Teresa jerked Clay through the door as he started toward the man.

"Come, *Señor* Best. He is not worth shooting. We shall stop farther down the road. *Dios* will give us a better place to say. You shall see."

"Maybe," Clay said as he helped her into the saddle. He jerked his gun back out of the holster as the door opened.

"Easy Pard, I ain't looking for no trouble." It was the man who had been sitting against the wall. He walked to a chestnut gelding and untied the reins.

"Ol' Luke had his wife and son killed by some banditos about six years back, and he's still nursing a grudge. I think he's a little worse every time I see him. It don't seem to make any difference. Male, female…he hates 'em all. It don't even matter how old they are. This woman could've been a baby, or someone's grandmother, and he'd have acted the same. He's festering away inside, and it's gonna kill him one of these days."

"We weren't looking for no trouble, mister."

"No, I never reckoned you were. Name's Allison." He shook Clay's hand. "You'll find a friendlier place a couple of miles up the road. It was started a year or so ago by an old *vaquero* named Guillermo, and he caters mostly to Mexicans and blacks. You might see a few Injuns every now and then, but they're mostly friendly. I'd rather stop there myself. Never liked Luke in the first place, and his whiskey's nothing but rotgut."

"Much obliged." Clay nodded.

"No problem. Hope you get to feeling better, ma'am." He touched the brim of his hat and galloped away toward Lehmann Ranch.

Clay turned Lucky toward the Anacacho Mountains and urged him forward at a walk as the bartender came to the door. Clay kept a wary eye on the man until he figured they were out of range, then increased their pace to a gentle trot.

"You should've let me turn that man's head into a pig trough," he finally said.

"What good would it do? He is only one, and there are many like him. Leave him alone. Some day he will need help, and there will only be Mexicans or black people or Indians. Then what will he do, *señor*? It is better to leave him alone."

~   ~   ~

Clay was still fuming a half-hour later when they came to a sprawling *jacale* with a corral and several horses tied to a fence. It wasn't the first time someone had been treated badly because their skin color or speech happened to be a little different from others. It hadn't been that long ago that Josefa Chipita Rodriguez had been hung for killing John Savage with an ax and dumping his body into the river. It was a murder that few believed she had actually committed.

The jury foreman during Josefa's trial had been the sheriff who arrested her, and three of the members were later indicted on felony charges unrelated to her trial. Josefa's only defense had been a "not guilty" uttered by her counsel. There was no appeal motion given. And while there had been rumors of a retrial, none took place. The trial angered a large number of residents, and Kate McCumber drove hangman John Gilpin off with a shotgun when he asked to borrow her wagon to transport Josefa to the hanging tree. At least one witness to the hanging claimed he later heard a moan from inside the coffin, which was placed in an unmarked grave and covered with dirt. Josefa had furnished travelers with meals and a cot on the porch of her lean-to shack on the Arkansas River for years prior, without a problem. The motive for the crime was said to have been the six-hundred dollars in gold that the victim had been carrying, but the money was found with the body.

Clay had met folks that claimed her ghost still haunts the area. They say she wanders the bottom land near the river with a noose around her neck, wailing for justice, but not finding any.

~   ~   ~

The cantina sat approximately thirty yards off the road. A small stream gurgled happily past the corral and toward the desert, to disappear somewhere in the sand and cactus. Clay tied their horses to the fence and helped Teresa from the saddle. She seemed weaker this time, as he helped her through the door toward a table. It took several seconds for his eyesight to adjust. There were five *vaqueros* leaning against the bar, with several more involved in a card game. The place grew quiet as Clay removed Teresa's sombrero and wiped the sweat from her eyes with his bandana.

"Hey, *hombre*, what is wrong with the woman?" the man behind the bar asked in a booming voice.

"Are you Guillermo?"

"*Si*, I am Guillermo." He rounded the bar and came toward them. "What do you want?"

"Allison told me to bring Mrs. Romero here, after that son-of-a-bitch down the road run us off. He said you would welcome us."

"Ah, *si*," he said with a nod. You should never have gone there, *hombre*. It is lucky he did not shoot you. He only likes people who are like him."

Teresa spoke rapidly in Spanish, and Guillermo's eyes darted back and forth between her and Clay before he grasped Clay firmly on the arm.

"*Si*, you are welcome here, *señor*. Sit." He motioned Clay to a chair next to Teresa's. "I shall get you and your woman something to drink." The place seemed to erupt into conversation as he rushed behind the bar. A man clad in sandals and a straw sombrero struck up a lively tune on a guitar and started to sing.

"What happened to her, *señor*," Guillermo asked, as he set two mugs of beer and two mugs of water on the table.

"She got shot a little over a week ago by a rustler, and almost bled to death. I reckon she ain't quite got her strength back, and the heat was getting to her. You got a place where we can bunk for the night?"

"*Si*, you are welcome to stay in my *casa*. It is not much, but it's better than the ground. You can put your horses in the corral out back. You'll find plenty of hay and everything you need. My Juanita is a good cook, I shall ask her to fix something for you."

Clay downed his beer in several gulps, then studied Teresa as she drank her water.

"Are you gonna be alright for a few minutes, while I take care of the horses?"

"*Si*." She smiled at him. "You go. I'll be okay."

~   ~   ~

He led the animals inside the corral and was in the process of unsaddling Loco when one of the *vaqueros* came through the door toward him. He gave Clay a friendly nod as he removed Diablo's saddle.

"This is a fine horse, *señor*. What is he called?"

"His name's Diablo. He belongs to Mrs. Romero."

"Ah, I think he must run like the devil." The *vaquero* ran a hand across Diablo's muscular shoulders and gave the animal a pat. The man was finely dressed with a high-brimmed sombrero and a tooled gunbelt. He had a brush knife tucked into his knee-high riding boots, as well as a large dagger hanging at his left side.

"Yeah, I've seen him run. He's the first hoss I've known that could give Loco a good chase." Clay patted Loco and turned toward the pack horse as the *vaquero* tossed several armfuls of hay into the trough.

"I am Julio Garcia. Your woman says you saved her life from the banditos who robbed the bank."

"Maybe." Clay led the pack horse to the feed-trough. There wasn't any need to tell him Teresa was not his woman, or that the rustler who had shot her had been a Mexican. "But I wasn't fast enough to save her from getting shot by the rustlers."

"What happened to the one who shot her?"

"I killed him."

"That is good. Come, I buy you tequila." He clasped Clay on the back as they walked back to the cantina.

~   ~   ~

Clay was halfway through a burrito filled with rice and beans when the door banged open and the owner of the trading post stormed inside. He had three other men with him. The larger of the three had a pot belly and a cheap-looking tin star pinned on his vest.

"That's him," Luke said, pointing toward Clay. "He had a gun and threatened to kill me and burn my place down. Arrest him!"

Clay laid his burrito on the plate and took a swallow of beer before standing. He couldn't remember his name, but he knew the potbellied man was a drifter who claimed to be a crackerjack of a lawman, although Clay had never seen any evidence to support the claim. "Na, I don't think I'm gonna let you arrest me today."

"Geeze, Luke," the fat man paled and backed away, "you didn't say it was Clay Best you wanted me to arrest."

"What difference does it make who he is, Ned? Arrest him!"

The four men glanced around them at the sound of scraping chairs and the cocking of weapons. Julio crossed the room to stand near the bar, giving himself the advantage of a crossfire.

"Ned," one of the men said, "that's Julio Garcia."

"I see him."

"Well, let's get the hell out of here."

"*Hombre,*" Guillermo said as he pointed a pistol toward Luke. "You say we are not welcome inside your place because we are Mexicans. I say okay and start my own cantina. Now you come here to arrest this man because he likes Mexicans? I think not. You have no right to come here and are not welcome."

"I'm not leaving without him." Luke pointed toward Clay.

"*Señor*," Teresa said as she calmly licked her fingers. "I saved your life once today." She laid one of the pearl-handled pistols on the table, "I will not do it again. Now leave while you are still alive, or I shall kill you myself."

The place erupted into hoots and whistles as the men backed through the door. Clay stood in the doorway and watched them climb on their horses.

~   ~   ~

"You crazy fool!" Ned said angrily. "I ain't coming on any more of your crazy hunts. Clay Best coulda killed all of us by himself. He doesn't need any help."

"Clay Best, Clay Best. Is that all you can say? I've never heard of the man before. Who in the hell is he?"

"You just go back in there, and you'll find out." Ned jerked his reins and spurred his horse into a run, scattering dust and bits of gravel as he left.

Chapter 31

"*Señor* Best?" Teresa abandoned the narrow bed and scooted against Clay who was lying on the floor. She leaned on her elbow to study his face. The pale moonlight from the window cast a soft glow across her nightgown, giving her slender body a subtle look as she tossed her leg across one of his. The sound of Guillermo's snoring through the heavy curtain almost drowned her whisper. She had been watching him sleep, trying to think of a way to describe what his very presence had meant to her, and what she was now feeling…but she found none.

She had always had a fear of being alone since she could remember. Her grandmother had said once that it had come from seeing the Comanches kill her father and mother, but Teresa could not remember the incident. The fear had grown worse with each passing year, until the demons came every night with the darkness to torment her. They came in many forms. Sometimes they were Comanches, with painted faces, screaming and killing. Her grandmother was alive and well when the Comanche demons came, and they would shoot their guns, but the demons kept coming, riding their horses up and down the road. When they had finally gone, she would run to hold Refugio's body in her arms. The Comanche lance had disemboweled her beloved Refugio, and one of the braves had taken his scalp. She wiped her palms against her nightgown, remembering the blood.

Other times, the demons came as the owner of the cantina. He and his friends would break down her door and come at her. She could hear Antonio barking, but could not see her beautiful dog, and his barks did not frighten the demons away. She would scream at them and shoot Refugio's pistol, but the bullets did not stop them as they did unspeakable things to her body. Teresa had found it easier not to sleep during the night, until the Holy Mother sent *Señor* Best into her life. He had chased the demons away with his presence, but she could not think of any way to tell him.

"*Señor* Best, are you awake?"

"If I wasn't, I am now. What is it?"

"You fought for me today, and I wish to thank you."

"You're welcome. Now, get some sleep. We have a busy day tomorrow."

"No," she grabbed his chin and forced him to look at her, "no one ever fights for me before."

"Oh, I'm sure boys used to fight over you all the time."

"*Si*, but no one defends my honor. No one protects me the way you do. I love you for doing it." She kissed him passionately before snuggling against his neck.

"*Buenas noches, mi amor.*" She heaved a sigh and drifted into a deep sleep almost immediately, leaving Clay wide awake.

"Yeah, good night," he whispered and ran a hand across her silky head.

Chapter 32

Uvalde lay 45 miles from Lehmann Ranch as a crow might fly, but the entire trip would cover 65 blistering miles, winding through the Anacacho Mountains. The barren, rocky hills sliced with limestone canyons and washes were dotted with shrubs and cactus, and climbed to a height of 1,316 feet. Clay figured it was a good place to break a leg on a horse, or get bitten by a rattlesnake. The occasional orchid tree that somehow seemed to thrive in the area was an oddity. The small tree grew to a height of twelve-feet and kept its leaves throughout the year. Following the spring rains, it sprouted pink and white blossoms which gave off a rich aroma. June used to tell him they were God's little reminder that He was still in charge. Clay figured that explanation fit as well as any he'd heard.

They walked their horses, covering some twenty miles the first day and stopping in Spofford. Clay bought extra canteens at the general store and filled them before leaving at daybreak the following morning. The road snaked around and through the rocks and canyons, weaving its way upward. The heat radiating from the boulders had begun to cook their skin by midday, making the tedious journey unbearable. Clay turned off the trail at mid-afternoon, where an orchid tree had found a sandy area to sink its roots, near several large boulders. Teresa's black blouse was coated with white, salty rings and she almost fell as she dismounted.

"Here, let me lend a hand," Clay said, leading her toward the shade. He grabbed one of the canteens and pulled the stopper. "Not too much now, just a few swallows."

"*Gracias.*" She obediently took a few sips and sat cross-legged with the canteen in her lap.

"You shoulda said something." Clay removed her sombrero and wet his handkerchief. She tilted her head back as he began washing her parched face. Her black curls were plastered against her pale cheeks and neck. She uttered a soft moan as he placed the damp cloth against the back of her neck.

"You'd better lay down." Clay positioned a folded saddle blanket behind her head and forced her back. "Don't do that to me again, you hear? When you start feeling faint, holler."

"But we need to find the *señorita,* and she's in San Antonio, *Señor* Best. She is not out here." She gave Clay a weak smile.

"We ain't gonna be finding anyone if you get sick and die on me. I should've waited a few more days at Guillermo's *cantina* before dragging you out here. You need to get some of your strength back. Now, I want you to tell me next time you start feeling puny. Understand?"

"*Si, Señor* Best. I will be a good girl."

Teresa closed her eyes and was asleep almost immediately. Clay unsaddled the horses and gave each a small amount of water and a portion of grain from a sack. Antonio came trotting in as he finished making camp. The dog looked exhausted, and finding a spot near his mistress, he went to sleep. Clay scrounged an armload of twigs and driftwood from one of the washes, then leaned back in the shade of a small boulder to smoke his pipe. He woke several hours later to the sound of clinking metal. Teresa had a small fire built and was making coffee. He glanced at the pipe lying next to him to discover it had gone out after only one or two puffs. He wiped the stem clean, propped it between his teeth and struck a match. There was no sense in letting good tobacco go to waste.

Chapter 33

The town of Cline was set on the bank of Turkey Creek, about eighteen miles west of Uvalde. The town found its humble roots when Celeste Pingenot arrived with a small herd of cattle in 1870 and built a home on the south bank of the creek. Being a man of vision, he established a stage depot a few years later, complete with stables and corrals. But Pingenot wasn't willing to let the Turkey Creek Stage Stop stand by itself. He built a store and saloon near his home, and followed them with the Wallace Inn, which he named after his friend, William (Bigfoot) Wallace, who brought the mail to the settlement. Turkey Creek, as the early settlers began to call it, became a popular stop for travelers on their way to Brackettville or to the silver mines in Mexico. Pingenot's greatest battle had come from Indians and Mexican bandits stealing his cattle and robbing an occasional incoming stage.

A post office was established in 1878, and Celeste Pingenot became postmaster. The settlement's name was officially changed to Wallace to match the Wallace Inn. A German named August Cline arrived in 1880 and became postmaster a year later, when the Texas and New Orleans Railroad was built. With the arrival of the railroad, Wallace became a thriving community of seventy-five and changed its name to Cline in 1883.

Clay and Teresa left their horses at Pingenot's stables and asked for a room at the Wallace Inn.

"You're in luck." Pingenot's wife, Minnie, flashed him a warm smile. "Several passengers got off the train an hour ago, but we still have one room available for you and your lovely wife. Please sign the register and I'll have Sophie make sure it's ready. She'll show you where the bath is and take care of you."

The room contained one bed, a small dresser and chair, a wardrobe, and lace curtains over the window. A braided rug covered the hardwood floor. Clay tossed their packs in one corner as Teresa sat on the edge of the bed and smiled.

"You did not tell the *señora* we are not married, *Señor* Best."

"No, I didn't. They only had one room available, and I figured there was no reason to raise anyone's hackles. We'll keep the same sleeping arrangements. I'll take the floor, and you can have the bed."

They bathed and ate a dinner of chicken and dumplings in the dining room. Clay made sure Teresa drank a large tumbler of milk, to help her regain her strength. He then gave Sophie their laundry and asked her to make sure Antonio got the table scraps, before retiring to their room. Teresa was already asleep when he made a pallet on the floor.

He woke early the following morning to the sound of boots against the wooden floor in the hallway. Teresa was lying next to him with her hair tickling his neck.

~   ~   ~

They spent the entire day sitting on the patio, soaking in the breeze and drinking a fair share of water. Teresa took a mid-afternoon nap in the room while Clay dozed in one of the patio chairs.

Teresa woke the following morning feeling energetic and restless, so Clay suggested they do some nosing around. They didn't have to go farther that the post office.

"Yes, I remember seeing her," August Cline said with a nod. "She arrived about two weeks ago on the train. She was here with a pretty nice fellow. In fact, they got married over at the church. Minnie and I witnessed the ceremony. They spent the night at the Inn and got back on the train the following morning on their way to San Antonio. Why are you looking for them? Did they do something wrong?"

"No, they didn't do anything wrong. Ruth and her grandpa had themselves a row, so she ran off and eloped. He just wants to make sure she's doing alright," Clay said with a shrug.

"They seemed pretty happy to me, but you'll need to find her in San Antonio if you want to ask her personally." August returned to sorting his mail and Clay took Teresa by the arm.

"I guess we'll be heading to San Antonio tomorrow. I reckon its safe enough to stable the horses here and take the train. I thought about it back at Lehmann's Ranch, but it's so close to the border, we would probably get back and find them missing. We can always rent a rig when we get there."

"*Si,*" she said. "Antonio and I have never ridden on a train."

Chapter 34

Clay believed San Antonio to be the epitome of Texas spirit. Located at the head of the San Antonio River, the city had its humble beginning in 1718, when five Spanish missions were established along the river. The town grew out of San Antonio de Béxar Presidio, and the villa of San Fernando de Béxar. By 1773 San Antonio de Béxar had become the capital of Spanish Texas. By 1778, its population had grown to a whopping 2,060, but its living conditions were described as being miserable. The residents consisted mostly of poor Europeans and a few black slaves. Spain decided to secularize all the missions in 1795, and San Antonio de Valero Mission became a military barracks. Then they changed its name to Alamo. San Antonio declared its independence from Mexico in 1813, but was recaptured by Mexico's Royalist forces and had its population decimated through several purges.

But true Texans never quit, and during the Texas Revolution, San Antonio was the site of several battles, including the siege of Béxar and the battle of the Alamo on March 6, 1836. The fact that San Antonio stood as one of the most fought-over cities in North America had become a badge of honor and a bragging-point for its residents. The city was a teeming, wealthy metropolis of more than 20,000 residents when Clay and Teresa stepped off the train. Teresa's mouth dropped open as she stood on the platform gawking at the mass of humanity before her. Clay grabbed their bags and tipped the porter before taking her arm.

A man leaned out of the baggage car as they passed and yelled, "Hey, mister, come get this dog. I ain't touching it. It's tried to bite me twice."

Traveling with Teresa had presented Clay with several challenges, one of them being Antonio. She had insisted on bringing the mongrel, but the animal was not permitted to ride inside the passenger car. Teresa had to coax him into the baggage car and into a caged-in area before they would allow them to board. Then the conductor had insisted on Teresa being seated in the rear of the car with other Mexican passengers. While the rule had caused Clay to clench his jaw, Teresa happily struck up a conversation with two women in Spanish, and chatted almost none-stop seventy miles to San Antonio.

Clay apologized for the dog's behavior, then waited until Teresa had fetched Antonio from the baggage car. The dog glanced back and growled one last time before leaping to the platform, where he wagged his tail and licked Teresa's hand repeatedly.

Clay heaved a sigh as he surveyed the frenzied activity around them. "Reckon we'd better hail a buggy, if one's to be found. We'll never find our way around here on our own."

~   ~   ~

The cabbie took them to a nice hotel and restaurant near the depot. Clay signed the register while Teresa made sure Antonio was put safely inside a fenced-in area at the rear of the hotel. They were escorted down a carpeted hall to a second story room. Clay ordered baths, and a brass tub, privacy screen and hot water were promptly brought to their room. Clay cleaned and oiled their guns while Teresa took her time soaking in the hot water. She came from behind the privacy screen fully dressed, and sat at the dresser braiding her long hair while Clay bathed.

They feasted in the restaurant on a meal of spicy beef, rice, beans and fresh bread, with fried apple turnovers for dessert. The coffee was good and hot, and they finished several glasses of red wine as they talked.

Teresa asked to see the sights, so Clay led her arm in arm from store to store, looking at the window displays. They stopped on a street corner on their way back to the hotel to let several carriages pass. Teresa leaned her head against Clay's chest.

"Oh, *Señor* Clay, it is so wonderful! I have never seen anything like it. I am very happy to be here with you."

"Yeah, I reckon it's something, alright. And I'm happy to be here with you too." He slipped an arm around her shoulder as they crossed the street.

"Wait," Clay said as they passed a shop window displaying gold and silver trinkets. "Come inside for a minute." He grabbed her hand and pulled her through the door.

"*Señor* Clay…? What are you doing?"

He motioned the young female clerk toward the window display and pointed toward a tiny silver cross on a delicate chain.

"Like it?" Clay asked, fastening it securely around her neck.

"*Si, si*, it is beautiful, but I already have a crucifix."

"Now you've got two." Clay paid for the necklace and they continued toward the hotel. They were almost at the front entrance when she pulled back and stared up into his face.

"Why did you buy the crucifix?"

"I just thought you'd like it. Besides," he stuffed his hands into his pockets and shuffled his boots uncomfortably. "You deserve something nice. You're a pretty nice lady."

"*Gracias*." She grabbed his shoulders with both hands and, bouncing to her tiptoes, she kissed him quickly on the mouth. "You are a nice man, *Señor* Clay." She took him by the hand and entered the hotel.

~　　　~　　　~

Clay woke the following morning lying next to Teresa in the same bed, wondering what June must be thinking. He was certain she was able to watch his every move from heaven, and probably didn't care that he and Teresa Romero hadn't done a blessed thing but sleep. He shouldn't be in bed with another woman, regardless of how innocent it might have been. What was worse, he couldn't put the blame on anyone but himself. She had tossed back the covers and smiled as she patted the mattress. Her white nightgown had ridden up over her knees, and didn't hide much as it clung to her slender frame. Clay stared at her briefly before sliding in next to her. She gave him a quick peck on the lips and whispered *"Buenas noches,"* as she snuggled close, then went to sleep.

He turned his head to study her profile against the white pillowcase. Her hair looked like raven waves cascading around her sculptured face. Teresa Romero was more than beautiful…she was gorgeous. June had also been a beautiful woman…much too good and pretty for the likes of him. Teresa certainly wasn't June, not by a long shot. She had a temper and could cuss a blue streak when riled. But she was honest and a good, loyal friend…someone you could count on when the cards were laid on the table. In short, he figured both women were beyond him. And while Teresa wasn't really his, and would eventually find someone else to fall in love with, he didn't know how in the hell he'd wound up with either woman.

Chapter 35

"Yes, I know Mrs. Stanley quite well. Her husband, Judge Stanley, is a good friend of mine." The bailiff leaned back in his chair still holding Ruth's picture. "What was your name again?"

"Clay Best, and this young lady is Teresa Romero." He glanced down at the name plate lying on the desk. "Look, Mr. Jenkins, you can't know Ruth all that well, since she married Judge Stanley only a few weeks ago. All we want is to ask her a few questions. We ain't looking to cause her any trouble."

The bailiff leaned forward and handed Clay the picture. "Mind telling me what this is about?"

"Her grandfather is looking for her," Teresa said quickly.

"That right? Then why didn't he just come?"

"Because, he doesn't know where she is, and he wants to make sure she's alright." Clay raised his voice, and several people in the lobby turned toward them. An elderly statesman grinned and crossed the room.

"Are we having a bit of trouble, Thad?

"No, Judge Stanley, but this couple keeps insisting they need to see Ruth."

"Hmm, that doesn't sound too difficult," he said with a chuckle. "May I ask why you wish to see my daughter-in-law?"

"As I've been trying to tell this knot-head, I'm Clay Best out of Cool Water, and this lady is Teresa Romero out of Carrizo Springs. Ruth's granddaddy, Lester Bishop, claims she just up and disappeared one day, and he's got himself a ransom note demanding $25,000 for her safe return. Now, me and Mrs. Romero figure Ruth might've eloped, and someone else is trying to collect on the old man's misery. That's what we aim to find out, if this joker will tell us where she is."

"You never said anything about any ransom note," Thad snapped.

"I'll handle this, officer Jenkins." The old man chuckled as he took Ruth's picture from Clay's hand. "You don't remember me, do you Marshal Best?"

"Can't say that I do."

"I'm Judge David Stanley, and you brought testimony against two men inside my court ten years ago, right in this very building. They had robbed a stage and killed the guard and the driver, and one of the passengers. You tracked them down and arrested both men. Your testimony was so convincing, the jury only deliberated six hours before finding the defendants guilty as charged. I had the pleasure of passing sentence, and seeing them hanged. Thank you again." He shook Clay's hand.

"Now I remember. You're a no-nonsense judge, who does things by the book. I reckon your boy might've followed in your footsteps?"

"Don't worry about Buford. You'd better be on your toes if you ever appear before him. As for me, I'm supposed to be retired, but they keep calling me back, for one reason or the other." He glanced at his pocket watch and passed Ruth's picture to Teresa.

"I believe Buford and Ruth should be home eating dinner about now. I'll take you to see them." He turned toward the bailiff and smiled. "Tell the court I am taking an early dinner break. I will hear their case when I return."

"Yes, Judge Stanley." Thad craned his neck and leaned across the desk as he watched them leave the building.

~   ~   ~

The judge called for his own carriage and chatted jovially as they wove their way through the busy San Antonio streets. The carriage came to a stop before an imposing two-story Victorian residence. Teresa couldn't contain a gasp.

"Yes, it is rather pretentious, isn't it?" Judge Stanley held Teresa's hand as she exited the carriage. "Edith and I still live in the same house we've lived in for the past thirty years. But young people today want the biggest and the best of everything Texas has to offer. They'd have a heart attack if they knew Sam Houston drank whiskey, smoked cigars, cussed and chewed tobacco inside his office."

He grabbed the knocker and rapped several times, then stepped back. The massive oak doors opened to reveal a Mexican woman dressed in black, wearing a white apron.

"On, *Señor* Stanley, your son will be so happy to see you. Please, you and your friends come, I will set a place for you at the table." She led the way toward the dining room, where Ruth met them as they entered. She caught her breath before rushing forward to give Clay a quick hug.

"Marshal Best…it's good to see you, but what in the world are you doing in San Antonio?"

"Do you know these people, dear?" Buford Stanley was a tall, gangly man. His eyes darted between Clay and Ruth as he rounded the table to greet them.

"Yes…yes I certainly do. I know Marshal Best. He was one of the true friends I had in Cool Water. I've cried on his shoulders many a time."

"Hello, I'm Buford Stanley." He gripped Clay's hand as his eyes darted toward Teresa.

"Oh, I forgot my manners. This young lady is Teresa Romero. She's a friend of mine who tagged along to keep me out of trouble."

"Have you actually been able to do that, Miss Romero? I mean, keep this man out of trouble?" Ruth raised her eyebrows and cocked her head.

"*Si*, but it is *Señor* Best who keeps me from getting hurt. He has saved my life twice since we met."

Ruth turned to watch as the maid rushed through the kitchen door to arrange three more place settings on the table, then rushed back into the kitchen.

"I'm afraid I'm the one who's forgetting her manners. Please," she motioned with her hand, "make yourselves comfortable. Yolanda works miracles in the kitchen…much better than I ever could. It's a wonder Buford stays so thin." Clay held a chair for Teresa and eyed Ruth across the table as she seated herself next to her husband. She had once been a skinny little thing who almost needed to be weighted down during a windstorm. While she still wasn't heavy, she had packed on a pound or two and looked as though married life was suiting her well.

Yolanda filled their plates with roast beef, mashed potatoes, garden-fresh green beans and hot biscuits. She returned seconds later with a pot of coffee and a pitcher of milk.

"Thank you, Yolanda," Ruth said as the woman left the room. She waited a second before giggling. "She insists that I drink several glasses of milk a day, and won't let me rest until I do." She folded her hands in her lap, smiling warmly at her father-in-law.

"Father, would you please ask the blessing?"

"I would be delighted to." The judge bowed his head and filled the room with his resonant voice as he asked for God's blessings on the food, on his family (especially his lovely daughter-in-law and future grandson), and finally on Clay and Teresa.

"*Gracias, señor*," Teresa said, crossing her breast. She took a sip of water, then smiled at Ruth. "When is your baby due, *señora*?"

"Baby?" Clay snapped his head around toward Teresa.

"*Si*, the *señora* is going to give her husband and papa a strong grandson or beautiful granddaughter. You did not know?"

Clay shook his head.

"And you are the one who was going to find her and discover the truth?" Teresa shook her head as she cut her meat. "It does not take much to know the *señora* is with child, *Señor* Best. It shows a little in her stomach," she motioned toward Ruth with her fork, "she drinks *leche*, and her father-in-law prays for his grandson who is not here. So, you tell me, don't you think *Señora* Stanley is having a baby?" She took a bite of roast beef and gave Clay a crooked grin.

Clay's eyes darted between the two women as they laughed.

"Yes, Marshal Best, I am going to have a baby. Now, perhaps you can tell me why you came all the way to San Antonio in this ungodly heat? I'm sure it has something to do with my grandfather, doesn't it?"

"Yes, the old goat thinks you've been kidnapped, so he sent me and Teresa to fetch you back to Cool Water. But I don't reckon you'd be willing to go, from the look of things. I can't say as I'd blame you."

"No, I'm afraid I wouldn't be willing to go, but why would he think I had been abducted? I simply wanted to get away from there, and he would never have allowed me to leave if I had told him."

"He has a note demanding money," Teresa said. "Show them, *Señor* Clay."

Clay dug the crumpled ransom note from his pocket and passed it across the table. Ruth read it slowly, then shook her head before handing it to her husband.

"I know nothing about this. I have no idea who could have written something like that. I simply needed to get away."

"It doesn't matter none," Clay said over a mouthful of potatoes. "I've got an idee who did it, and I plan to discuss things with them when we get back to Cool Water."

"But, why did *you* come?" Ruth wrinkled her brow. "I thought you had quit working for my grandfather. That was the main reason I left. After June died…and I watched you ride away, I knew the very last friend I had left was gone. I was alone, Marshal Clay. I didn't have a soul I could actually talk to, who would be there and understand when I needed to cry.

"And I'd hated grandfather so much, for what he did to Billy, cheating him out of that money and running him out of town, simply because he loved me. Oh, I know Billy Mayfield was a scoundrel," she shook her head, "but he did love me, and treated me like a lady…which was something grandfather never did. Then Billy got killed trying to get the money grandpa owed, and the only friends I had left were you and June." She shrugged.

"There were others," Clay said as he buttered a biscuit. "How about Sarah Walker and Louise Kirkland? They were pretty good friends, weren't they?"

"Yes, they certainly were. But they were silly girls like myself, and you couldn't really tell them things in secret. My grandfather would have known everything if I had told them." Ruth took a sip of milk and smiled sadly.

"After you left, Benjamin Rogers started playing up to me, and I let him. He said he loved me, and he promised to take me away. He wanted to elope. Being a romantic girl, I believed him. I packed my clothes and we left in the middle of the night." She heaved a deep sigh. "Benjamin was a drunk who beat me. He was mean and vicious…and gambled away my last cent. I wouldn't be surprised if he had something to do with that note. I hate to admit it, but I was actually happy when that old man killed him. To complicate things, I woke up to discover I was going to have a baby." She covered her mouth and choked back a sob.

"Then I met Buford. He knows all about me and my baby, and…" she broke into sobs, "he still loves me. Can you believe it? The whole family knows, and they love me!"

Clay felt his own eyes water as Buford Stanley hugged his wife. Teresa dropped her fork and covered her mouth with her napkin as she burst into tears. David Stanley squeezed Teresa's hand and smiled proudly at his son and daughter-in-law.

"Well, I reckon that tells me everything I needed to know," Clay said after Ruth had calmed herself. "I'll mosey back toward Cool Water in the morning, and give your grandpa your regards. You wouldn't have some sort of announcement about your getting hitched I could take? Just so the old man will know I ain't lying. He's paying me to do this, or I wouldn't be here otherwise." He glanced at Teresa as she cast an angry glare his way. "Not to say I wouldn't find you on my own, but I wouldn't have bothered telling that miserable grouch anything. Besides, this woman threatened to shoot me if I didn't make sure you were alright."

"I have several copies of the newspaper with the marriage announcement in my office. You may have one to give Ruth's grandfather, if you wish," David said as he poured himself a glass of milk. He held the glass high. "To you my dear daughter. You are the best thing that has ever happened to my son. And to my grandson, who will become the most loved and spoiled brat in Texas."

"But what if the baby is a *niña*?" Teresa asked.

"Even better. I will personally see to it that my granddaughter becomes the most celebrated young woman in Texas history."

Chapter 36

Clay removed his coat and tie, and tossed both across the back of a chair. Teresa came from behind the privacy screen and placed her carefully folded clothes inside her pack. Clay watched as she passed in front of the lamp, then turned away. Watching her silhouette through the nightgown had become a habit he would have to break. He was beginning to entertain thoughts about Teresa that could be dangerous. He was a good fifteen years older than her, and figured she would be moving on once the right fellow came along.

"So, tell me *Señor* Clay, what do we do now?" She sat on the edge of the bed with her hands folded in her lap. Her long hair framed her face and hung across each shoulder, making her seem like an innocent child.

"Well, I reckon we take that newspaper to Lester and ask to get paid."

"Do you think he will be happy for his granddaughter?"

Clay laughed as he removed his boots.

"No, I reckon he's gonna pitch a fit. He's gonna balk at paying us, but I figure we can't do anything else. I certainly ain't gonna kidnap Ruth and haul her back to Cool Water. That'd be like sending her to hell. Besides, if he wants to try talking her into moving back, he can come to San Antonio and twist Judge Stanley's arm his own self."

"*Bien*," she said with a nod. She tossed the covers back and crawled in the bed. She sat with her arms wrapped around her knees, smiling as Clay unbuttoned his shirt. He stopped to stare back, then turned away.

"You'd best be looking the other way, or at least blow out the lamp." He tossed the shirt on top of his jacket.

"*Por que*? Why must I look the other way?"

"Because it ain't proper."

"Who says such a thing? I like watching you undress. Besides, I never see anything but your underthings. You never remove them for me."

Clay turned around so quickly it made her laugh.

"What would be wrong with seeing your body, *Señor* Clay? You see my breast when I am shot, and *Dios* did not strike you dead."

"That was different, and you know it." He pointed his finger at her. "Now, blow out the lamp and look the other way."

"As you wish." She giggled and blew out the lamp. "I am looking at the wall, *Señor* Clay. You may finish undressing and come to bed."

"I shouldn't even be doing this," he said as he crawled in next to her. His heart almost stopped as she quickly rolled, pressing her body against his. He could feel the swell of her breast as she breathed against his ear.

"I love teasing you, *Señor* Clay. You are like a little *niño*. You blush easy. We do nothing wrong, and it would not bother me seeing your body with no clothes. I find you pretty, the same as you find me pretty."

"Teresa…"

"No," she silenced him by placing a finger against his lips. "I see how you watch me, especially when I am in my nightgown. It does not bother me. I like it when you find me pretty. And it is enough that we are friends for now. Some day we will share more, but that is for later." She shifted to hover inches over his face, her hair caressing his cheeks. He caught his breath, assuming she was going to kiss him on the lips, but she instead tickled him, and rolled over laughing.

"You little devil." Clay grabbed for her ribs, causing her to squeal. When someone in the adjoining room pounded against the wall, Teresa covered her mouth to smother another fit of giggles, then slipped an arm around Clay's neck and kissed him long and tenderly before snuggling her head against his chest.

"*Buenas noches, mi compañero.*"

Clay stared into the dark room, not seeing anything. It only took a matter of minutes before the rhythm of Teresa's soft breathing told him she had fallen asleep. *Good God, what have I done?* He had never expected anything like this to happen. When he had asked June to marry him, he had pledged there would never be another woman…ever. And he still meant every single word. But Teresa was making him feel and think very differently. He would have to put a quick end to this relationship, once they had finished their dealings with Lester Bishop. He might have to move completely out of the area, perhaps leave Texas altogether. He'd heard rumors that California was nice. Maybe that's where he'd go. Anywhere that Teresa Romero *wasn't* would be a good place.

Chapter 37

They ate a quiet breakfast at the hotel, then boarded the train. Clay stared out the window, deep in thought. Teresa passed the time chatting in Spanish with a heavyset woman. It was hot, and several passengers opened their windows. The air blowing in was smoky and felt like an oven. Teresa finally tired of talking and fell asleep against Clay's shoulder. She woke as the train slowed in its approached to the Cline depot.

"Did you have a nice nap?" Clay asked, as she sat up and began fussing with her hair.

"*Si, gracias.* What time is it?"

Clay checked his watch. "Three-thirty, if my watch is correct. The train's running about fifteen minutes behind."

Clay collected their belongings as Teresa rescued Antonio from the baggage car. They walked leisurely back to the Wallace Inn and checked into their room. Clay removed his boots and flopped on the bed with a grunt as Teresa grabbed a fresh change of clothing and headed toward the bath. He was snoring loudly when a pair of soft lips kissed him on the cheek.

"Huh?" He jerked up with a start.

"It is growing late, *Señor* Clay, and people have arrived on the stage. You must go to the *baño* now, if you want to wash before dinner."

"Mmm, yeah. Thanks." Clay rubbed a hand across his face and slipped his boots on. He grabbed a few things and glanced over his shoulder as he opened the door. Teresa was humming a tune as she brushed her hair in front of the mirror. He shuffled down the hall, wondering how in the hell she had gotten in the habit of bathing so often. Worse yet, how she had gotten *him* into the habit. It must be bad on a person's skin to scrub that much. He'd have to ask Doctor Adams about it the next time he wandered through Eagle Pass. Besides, there was a drought on, and some poor cow was probably wandering around thirsty because that woman used up all the drinking water scrubbing good Texas dirt off herself.

Chapter 38

They took their time crossing the Anacacho Mountains. That night they camped under the same orchid tree they had camped under on their way to Cline. They reached the desert floor the following afternoon and turned in a more southerly direction, hoping to cut down on the travel and save the horses. Making camp near a small trickle of a stream with alkali-tasting water, Clay built a fire and hobbled the horses while Teresa cooked a supper of salt pork, stale tortillas and dried fruit.

"Not half-bad, considering what you had to work with," Clay said after choking down the last of his tortilla. "I thought about shooting a jackrabbit, but it's too hot, and the danged thing would probably be wormy."

Teresa stared at him with part of a tortilla halfway to her mouth.

"I did not need to hear that, *señor*."

"Come on, you've heard worser things than that, and probably eaten worse than a gamey rabbit."

"Maybe, but not by choice. I shall fix *carne y ensalada* when we get home. And we shall have tequila." She finished with a firm nod as she shoved the remaining bite inside her mouth.

"Well, we might not have fresh steak and tortillas," Clay said as he got to his feet, "but I can solve part of our problem." He rummaged inside one of the saddlebags, producing a small bottle of tequila. He pulled the cork and poured a shot into her cup.

"*¿Qué?* You are a man of many surprises, *Señor* Best." She smiled and took a sip.

"I suppose I might have a card or two up my sleeve. Here's to the prettiest saddle partner I've ever had." He toasted Teresa and downed his tequila.

"And here's to the only saddle partner I've ever had." Teresa downed her tequila and smiled.

"I thought you said you had ridden with your husband a time or two."

"*Si,* but when I ride with him, he spends more time talking with Heraclio Bernal than with me. I was told to stay back with the putas they had with them, and not get hurt, or say anything or cause trouble. I was there, but I did not like it much. I only saw my Refugio at night when he wanted to make love, or go to sleep." She stared into the empty cup and shrugged. "I felt like a whore, more than his wife."

He poured another shot into each cup and leaned back against his saddle to watch the fire.

"Well, it's certainly been different on this ride. We've kept each other company the entire time."

"Did you mind having my company, *Señor* Best?"

"No…no, I didn't mean it like that. But, I suspect you might be getting a little tired of me by now." He chuckled and took a sip.

"No, no, no," Teresa said, scooting close and laying her head against his shoulder. She kissed him on the cheek. "Don't ever think that. You are my big, strong angel, and you take care of me. I feel safe with you."

"Well, I don't reckon I've been called an angel before. I've done things, Teresa. I've killed men and seen things I don't reckon you ever should. I might not be the kind of person you should be hanging around with. I certainly wasn't the type of husband June needed to have underfoot."

"*No es importante, nosotros no somos casados.*"

"Huh? I don't reckon I caught all that."

"Oh," she shifted around to smile inches from his face, "I say it is not important, we are not married." She slipped an arm around his neck and kissed him on the mouth.

Teresa finished her tequila and lay with her head in his lap, talking and gazing at the stars. Antonio wandered into camp looking tired but satisfied. He gave her a lick on one cheek and curled up next to the fire to sleep. Clay woke the following morning with Teresa snuggled close. She had one leg draped across his middle, and her face buried against his chest. Feeling a desperate need to visit the nearest clump of bushes, he tossed the blanket off, but quickly jerked it back on. The nightgown had ridden up to her waist during the night, and Teresa wasn't wearing any unmentionables. Clay had gotten a good look at one bare leg and a shapely hip.

Now, that's a hell of a thing to see first thing in the morning. He fell back against his saddle and stared into the early morning sky. The urge to visit the brush had suddenly vanished.

Chapter 39

"Well, this is going to take some work." Clay pushed his hat to the back of his head and looked at the clump of cactus that had been Teresa's target. She had missed it by three feet. They had traveled due south, and were about a day from reaching Carrizo Springs when Clay decided it was time Teresa had a little training.

"I do not shoot well with my left hand, *Señor* Best." She stared at the gun in her hand.

"I can believe it. But you'd better learn well enough to be tolerable. What are you going to do if you ever get winged in the right arm again, or fall off a horse and bust your arm in the middle of a battle? This ain't no game you're playing. There's men and women out there who are just plain mean, and they won't care none if you're a good-looking woman, or a nice one. They'll kill you just for standing there. Now, try it again."

Teresa aimed and squeezed the trigger. The bullet clipped the tip of one branch of the cactus.

"Not bad…that was much better," Clay said. "Now hit that same branch dead center."

It took her three more tries, but the third bullet penetrated the branch almost dead center.

"Very good. Now, let me see you reload with one hand."

Her eyes darted between the pistol and Clay several times.

"*¿Qué*, how am I supposed to do that, *Señor* Best? Why can't I use my other hand? It is much better. See?" She swung her arm in an arch and wiggled her fingers in his face.

"I know it is." He gave a nod. "But I told you to do it. Now, let's see you reload using only one hand."

"You told me?" She raised her voice and glared. Her heart leaped as he jerked the .45 from his holster and fired three times quickly, causing chunks of the cactus to fly with each shot. He flipped the gun to his left hand and fired three more times, hitting the cactus with each shot.

"That's just so you'll know I can do what I'm asking you to do." He held the gun in his left hand with the barrel pointed upward, rotating the cylinder with his fingers and allowing the empty shell-casings to fall. He tucked the gun under his right arm, pulled bullets from his belt, and reloaded with his left hand as he talked.

"I reckon you getting shot back there was mostly my fault. When I seen you kill Joe Donaldson that day, I took it for granted you was handy with a gun. Then when you told me you and your husband had both ridden with Heraclio Bernal, and when I seen you handle yourself back at that wash, pulling the horses to one side and moving off to my right...Well, I just took you for a genuine pistolero and figured you didn't need any teaching." He finished reloading and holstered his pistol.

"Now that I've had some time to think about it, that ain't so. You might know the drill well enough, and can handle yourself real good up to a point. But knowing how to position yourself and how to shoot are only a small part of keeping yourself alive. You had the drop on that man back there, and let him shoot you."

"But *Señor* Clay..."

"No, let me finish." He took the .38 from her hand and reloaded it. "When you killed Donaldson, that was simply due to you being plenty mad, but anger ain't enough, and it sometimes gets in the way. Men like Hickock, King Fisher, or Sam Bass figure the man they're facing is dead before they even pull their gun. They don't blink or hesitate. They pull their gun and shoot in one motion. So," he handed her the loaded .38, "you'll only have a half a second to decide whether or not to pull the trigger and send whoever it is into eternity, or you'll end up dead."

"But, I didn't know that man would shoot. I just think he will drop his rife and…"

"The thing is, he didn't. And you got shot. Understand that?" He almost yelled, and she cowered backward.

"You talked me into taking you on this wild-goose hunt, when I didn't think Ruth Bishop was kidnapped in the first place. But we went, and you almost got yourself killed. Now, even if I never take you on another one of these trails, you need to learn to stay alive. So you'd best do what I say, and do it when I say. And no arguing or you'll never saddle up with me again. Do you understand me?"

"*Si*, I understand, *Señor* Clay."

"Good, now start practicing, using both hands." Clay dug Refugio's pistol from Teresa's pack and aimed it at the cactus. The hammer fell with a loud click. He repeated the action and only one of the six chambers fired.

"Aren't you glad you didn't try using this thing against Donaldson? We'd both be dead. A gun like this needs to be emptied and reloaded every day. I'll have it re-chambered to hold .45s when we get back to Carrizo Springs, that way you won't have to worry about it."

Chapter 40

Teresa drank too many cups of coffee with her supper and woke in the middle of the night with an urge to visit a clump of greasewood brush. She sat upright, quietly wrapping the blanket around her shoulders as the chill of the night air hit her. She glanced toward Clay, rolled snuggled in his bedroll, not more than six inches away. *When I return, I will share my blanket with you, mi amor. I know you do not like it, but it is mucho frío tonight.*

Antonio perked his ears at the rustle of the blanket and came to stand beside her as she pulled on her boots without any stockings. She had begun the habit of sliding under the blankets next to Clay in the middle of the night simply because she found him comfortable, and his presence chased away the bad dreams. But now she found herself snuggling close to his warm body on nights when the bad dreams had not come. He would growl at her in the morning and tell her that for them to sleep in the same bed did not look right. He would tell her it didn't matter whether or not they had committed sin; God would not like it. But she knew he enjoyed being near her as much as she enjoyed being with him. It was something she could feel inside, regardless of his growling like an old dog.

She knew Clay Best loved her. It had come to her the day the fat man had burst into Guillermo's cantina, demanding the arrest of *Señor* Clay. She had suddenly realized how much she loved him in return. Up to that point, she had thought of him as a good friend, enjoying his companionship, but now, she couldn't picture herself without him. He was part of her life, and he treated her with respect, even when she made him angry. That was something no man had ever done. Even Refugio had slapped her a few times in anger. But Clay had never lifted a finger, even when she had made him furious. Most importantly, she knew he never would. It was simply not in him to treat a woman that way. It was also true that he had never made any romantic advances toward her. *But Señor Clay will love me the same way. I know he will.*

She pulled the blanket tightly against her shoulders and rose quietly, then paused to pull one of the .38's from the holster, in case of snakes or coyotes. After a gentle pat on the head, Antonio followed her into the bushes to stand guard. Teresa could still hear Clay's peaceful snoring as she hiked up the gown.

She was ready to return to her bed when Antonio perked his ears and emitted a low growl. Teresa squatted next to the dog, laying a hand against the back of his neck.

"Shhhh," she whispered softly. "What is it?" That was when she heard the sound of a boot crunching against the gravel, followed by a whispered curse. Teresa slipped silently from the greasewood to squat behind a large clump of cactus for a better view. Two dark figures stood silhouetted against the desert landscape in the moonlight. Clay stirred slightly on the opposite side of the cactus, but remained asleep. The figures moved their heads slightly from side to side, as though they were surveying the camp, then one of them nodded to the other. Satisfied that they had not disturbed anyone, they crept closer, hunching over. Both men carried rifles, and one of them motioned toward his partner to move farther toward his right. Antonio's second growl caused both men to freeze. Teresa stroked the dog's neck to quiet him as she gripped the pistol in her left hand and slowly cocked the hammer. She glanced to where Clay was lying. He stirred once again, but didn't wake up.

The men were now approaching the campfire that had died down to a bed of red coals. At this point both men slowly raised their rifles. Teresa released her hold on Antonio and yelled.

"*¡Consígalos* Antonio! Get them!" The dog rounded the clump of cactus in three bounds, leaping through the air as the men jerked around. One of them screamed as Antonio struck his chest, knocking him to the ground. The second man raised his rifle just as Teresa fired. Her bullet spun him completely around and he fell.

"*¡*Antonio, *La parada, viene aquí!* Come here. Good boy." Clay was suddenly on his feet beside her with a pistol in his hand.

"Naw, you just lay there," he said, and kicked the rifle away. "Come on now, let's have the hogleg. Nice and easy," he added as the man reached for his pistol.

"You too," he said to the other. "Nice and easy, or I'll send you to hell without a prayer."

The man tossed his handgun halfway to Clay with his left hand.

"Okay, you highbinders, get on your feet." He gestured toward both men with his .45.

"I'm shot and bleeding," the second one complained as he struggled to his feet. "We were just gonna take your poke. You didn't have to shoot me."

"That ain't likely. But I didn't shoot you. You'd be dead if I'd drilled you. This woman did, and she's more generous than I am."

"Geeze almighty!" The first man staggered to his feet. "Keep that animal away from me," he added as Antonio growled. His shirt hung in shreds, revealing several bloody wounds on his arms and left cheek.

"Hey, *hombre*," Teresa motioned toward the one she had shot. "How bad are you hurt?"

"You shot me. How in the hell do you think I am?" He grimaced as blood seeped through the fingers that were pressed against his right shoulder.

"I did not shoot to kill you, so answer me *hombre*, or I'll shoot you again."

"Hell, I don't know how bad it is." He glanced at the wound. "It hurts…that's all I know."

"It's supposed to hurt, you numbskull," Clay growled. "Now unbuckle your belts and drop them."

"You've already got our guns," one of them complained.

"Now I want your belts," Clay said, and rapped him across the shoulder with his gun. The man staggered backward with a cry of pain. "Come on, I want your belts. You've both got knives, and no telling what else on you. Nice and easy. I said nice and easy," he added as the one he had struck reached for the buckle.

"Now, get over there by the fire and let's have a look at you. Both of you." He motioned with his pistol.

Teresa stoked the fire and Clay waited until it was casting a warm glow against the night before ordering the men to sit cross-legged in the sand. Teresa tossed the men's weapons beside her blankets and stepped behind a bush to slip into her riding skirt. She laid the folded nightgown on her bedroll and rummaged through one of the packs for bandages, but stopped to cock her head and give Clay a puzzled look. "You were awake, *señor*?"

"Sure. I don't sleep quite that sound. I knew when you got up and I heard them coming."

"But you were making the noise…the…the…"

"I was snoring?"

"*Si*," she said with a nod and fished a pack of bandages from the bag.

"Well, I admit to that. But I figured if I stopped, it would've tipped these two off and they would simply have stood back and bored us with those Winchesters."

"Hum." She made her way toward the wounded man.

"Okay, *hombre*, let me see how bad I shoot you. Sit quietly and don't touch me, unless you want *Señor* Clay to shoot you. He will do a much better job than I do."

She ripped open the shirt and dabbed at the wound with a rag.

"S*eñor*, I am afraid I only scratch you with my bullet, yet you cry like a little baby. You sit here while I see how bad Antonio treats your friend."

"I'm still bleeding, dammit! Do something!"

"Hush your mouth," Clay growled. "Feel lucky she only grazed your shoulder. I heard y'all coming and was fixing to kill you when she sicced the dog on your friend." He fished a bottle of tequila from his bag and uncorked it.

"Hold on a second," he said, as Teresa prepared to wrap the arm that Antonio had chewed. Clay poured a generous amount of tequila over the wound. His partner laughed as the man howled in pain. Clay took a swig from the bottle and promptly poured some over the laughing man's shoulder, for which he received a howl, mingled with several curses.

"Hush! You're gonna embarrass Mrs. Romero."

~ ~ ~ ~

Clay tossed more wood onto the fire and made a pot of coffee while Teresa tended to the wounds. The sun had begun to turn the eastern sky pink by the time she had finished, and she sat on her blankets cross-legged as Clay poured her a cup of coffee.

"Where's your hosses?"

"Back in the brush thatta way." The larger of the two motioned with his head.

"Get on your feet. You and me's gonna take a little walk and fetch them. And you," Clay eyed the second one carefully, "what's your name?"

"I'm Josh Miller and he's Curley Paulson. Look, we're plumb broke, mister. This is the first time we've tried something like this. We've been looking for work, but there ain't any work nowhere. And we ain't ate in several days."

"Well, I'll tell you what Josh, you keep sneaking up on folks at night and trying to rob them, and you won't be eating ever again. Folks get killed doing things like that. If you wanted a bite to eat, all you had to do was holler and walk in here nice and peaceful-like and this woman would've fed you. Now, your partner and me is gonna fetch your horses. I'd advise you to sit there and don't try anything funny. Teresa's plenty handy with a pistol and she ain't afraid to use it. Besides," he snickered, "Antonio ain't had his breakfast yet, and he's already had a taste of you."

Teresa ordered Antonio to stand guard over her prisoner as she brushed her hair. Clay grinned as the dog trotted over to hold his large snout inches from Josh Miller's face.

"Okay, let's go." He motioned Curley ahead of him.

"What are you gonna do with us?"

"I ought to kill you both for disturbing our sleep. But, we'll feed you breakfast and take you into Carrizo Springs. The rest will be up to Sheriff Ray King. He'll probably hand you over to the Rangers for trial, and they'll more'n likely lock you up for awhile, but you'll be getting fed twice a day."

Chapter 41

They arrived in Carrizo Springs late that afternoon, hot, tired and dusty. Clay turned their prisoners over to Sheriff King before unloading their packs at the gate as Teresa went to check on the house. He took the horses to Miguel's stables and walked back, feeling wrung-out. He stood in the shade of the willow, staring at the small *jacale*. It didn't belong to him, but it felt good to be back. Teresa had already moved the packs to the front porch and had water heating on a fire in the front yard. She was shooing a wayward hen out the door with her broom as he closed the gate. He suddenly felt like he had come home.

"I see you already moved our grip."

"*Si*, I already start unpacking."

"Was the place a mess?" he asked, swatting at the dust on his clothing.

"No, I think Juanita comes and cleans when they feed the chickens. There is a little dust, but that is okay. I will have bath water ready in *un minuto*. You sit and remove your boots."

"Nope," Clay shook his head, "any Texan worth his salt will let a woman go first. You sit and remove your boots." He rummaged in the cupboard until he found a bottle of brandy and two glasses. He blew the dust from the glasses and filled them. "Drink this while I fetch your bath water."

"Mmm," Teresa said as she took a sip. "You will spoil me if you are not careful, *Señor* Clay."

"Well, you've cooked for me and waited on me the past two months. I might as well return the favor." He paused at the door and snickered. "Only thing is, I'm a real lousy cook. I burn most everything."

"I will cook for you, after I finish my brandy and take a bath." She toasted him with her glass and smiled.

~ ~ ~

Clay was soaking in the tub and using a hand-held mirror to shave his whiskers, when he heard Teresa squeal inside the house. He reached for the towel, but relaxed as he heard her laughing. He had just finished with the razor when Miguel slipped in past the curtain with two small cups of tequila and a salted lime.

"Here, *amigo*. This is to celebrate your return." He passed one of the cups and a slice of lime to Clay. "It is good to see you back. I wasn't in town when you bring the horses, but they are taken care of."

"I wasn't worried. Your oldest boy, Juan, was rubbing them down when I left. Salud." Clay toasted Miguel and downed his tequila.

Miguel took the empty cup and tossed the towel at Clay.

"You'd better get dressed, *señor*. Juanita has cooked and it will get cold if you wait too long."

"Huh," Clay said as Miguel closed the curtain, "That ain't likely. My stomach thinks my throat's been cut." He quickly dressed and hurried into the house to find Miguel and Juanita, their six children, and Teresa patiently waiting.

"It is a good thing you arrived, *Señor* Clay. Jose was ready to eat all the food." Teresa grinned and pinched Juanita's youngest son on the nose.

"Just so long as y'all saved a little for me, that's all I ask." Clay pulled up a chair as Juanita slid a plate in front of him piled with beans, rice, hot tortillas, and shredded pork covered with green chili sauce. "Lord have mercy, I think I've died and gone to heaven."

"Before you make a pig out of yourself," Teresa said as she poured the wine, Miguel and Juanita always pray for *Dios* to bless the food."

"Huh…oh, yeah," Clay laid his fork back on the table and bowed his head. He looked up when Miguel had finished praying, to see Teresa smiling at him across the table.

"You may make a pig of yourself now, *señor*. No one will care."

"That's good." He scooped a forkful of beans into his mouth. "I might've had to shoot someone otherwise."

Chapter 42

Clay decided to relax a couple of days before taking the ten-mile ride to Cool Water. He wasn't looking forward to seeing Lester Bishop anytime soon, although the thought of telling the old bastard they had found Ruth, and she didn't want to ever see him again, brought a little satisfaction. But the horses needed the rest and besides, he was tired of traveling. He was sitting on Teresa's front porch enjoying a strong cup of coffee when she came outside wearing a straw sombrero, with both pistols hung on her hips. The shopping basket filled with wild flowers hanging on her arm seemed somehow out of place.

"Come, *Señor* Clay. I show you where Refugio is buried."

"Sure." Clay tossed the remnants of the coffee in the yard and took her arm like a gentleman. She led him past the cantina toward the Catholic church at the end of the wide street. Several heads turned to stare, and Clay chuckled.

"What is funny, *Señor* Clay?"

"Oh, I just realized what those folks were gawking at. I reckon we must make a sight. We're both dressed in black, and we're toting hardware like hired guns, yet you're carrying flowers."

"Maybe we go to a funeral and I bring the flowers."

"Most folks don't take guns to funerals."

"They do if they wish to make sure the person is dead."

She started laughing as he stopped to look down at her.

"You had me going there for a minute." He smiled. "That was actually good. I'll have to remember that one."

She led him past the church to a small fenced-in cemetery. Several graves were decorated with the dried stems of flowers and an occasional strand of rosary beads or a crucifix draped over a marker. Teresa stopped beside a mound of dirt with a simple wooden cross and removed her sombrero, allowing it to hang against her back by the braided drawstring. She squatted on her heels, placing several wild poppies near the marker.

"This is where my Refugio is, *Señor* Clay. He has been gone two years now, and I think of him fondly. And this," she split the remaining flowers between two graves next to Refugio's, "is where my grandmother Yolanda sleeps, and grandpapa lies next to her. She is dead only eight months now, and I miss her."

She crossed her breast and began praying in Spanish. Clay removed his hat and waited, then offered his hand when she had finished.

"It takes awhile, getting over someone dying on you, doesn't it?"

"*Si, Señor* Clay," she sniffed and dabbed at her eyes, "and it hurts. But you will have fond things to remember." She took his arm as they headed back toward town.

"I shall always remember my grandmother teaching me to cook, and how to dance. Every time I make *nopales* I think of her."

"I reckon that's the way it's supposed to be."

They stopped at the market, where Teresa carefully picked fresh peppers, tomatoes and cilantro, along with several more items she needed to restock her kitchen. They were passing the cantina when a huge man, wearing a filthy apron and a sweat-stained shirt, came through the door and tossed a bucket of dirty water into the dusty street. He turned toward Clay and snorted.

"Well, I see she's got you keeping her bed warm. How do ya like her? She's pretty good, ain't she?" He had no more gotten the words out when Clay knocked him to the ground. The bartender flung the heavy wooden bucket, and Clay batted it away with his forearm as he moved quickly toward the man.

The bartender scrambled to his feet cursing. He was several inches taller than Clay, and outweighed him by a good twenty pounds. Clay faked a blow to his face, causing him to raise his hands, then kicked him hard in the kneecap. The bartender howled as he bent forward, grabbing for his wounded leg. Clay hit him several times, driving him to the sidewalk. He caught a glimpse of Teresa from the corner of his eye as she dropped her shopping basket and jerked one of the pistols from her holster. His initial response was to stop her from killing the man, but he froze when he discovered a second man had come from the cantina, carrying a shotgun, which was pointed toward him. Teresa shoved the .38 against the back of the man's neck and cocked the hammer.

"Go ahead *señor* and see what happens. You shoot *Señor* Clay and I will kill both of you. Believe me *hombre*, it will not make me sad one little bit to shoot you."

Chapter 43

Sheriff Ray King woke feeling relaxed and peaceful. Maria had put the twins to sleep early and come to bed feeling playful. He couldn't remember actually falling asleep. He only remembered being somewhere in heaven with the prettiest angel wrapped in his arms. He crawled out of bed and dressed to the sound of Maria's humming, mingled with clanking dishes and the smell of coffee. She smiled warmly as he slipped his arms around her waist and kissed her ear.

"*Buenos días, el marido*. Your breakfast is ready. Get our coffee and I will get the boys."

Ray poured two steaming mugs and slid them on the table before scooping one of the twins from the floor as he darted past. "Whoa there, partner. Your ma has chuck all ready for us. You'd better eat your fill before you head out chasing bad *hombres*." Maria came from the bedroom carrying the other, who still had not fully wakened. He kissed her again as she adjusted herself at the table. He had found the perfect wife.

They enjoyed a leisure breakfast and lingered over several cups of coffee. Then he heaved a sigh as he checked his watch. He was already a half an hour late for making his rounds, not that he figured it mattered. The town mostly ran itself these days.

Ray kissed her and the boys once again and donned his favorite hat. He strolled casually down the sidewalks, greeting people as he passed. It was a beautiful morning. The hammer inside Roy Johnson's blacksmith shop sang a merry tune as several barefoot boys played tag with a barking dog in the street. The warm sun had not yet turned to a baking heat, and the day promised to be a pleasant one. Spying Clay and Teresa walking arm in arm, Ray decided to cross the street and ask if they had had any luck finding the Bishop girl. The subject had completely slipped his mind when Clay had given him the two prisoners. He was in the middle of the street when Hugh Tullis came out of the cantina and tossed a bucket of water into the street. "Aw, hell," Ray muttered as he increased his stride. There had been bad blood between the man and Mrs. Romero. He had never learned what had started the feud, but he'd heard some of the rumors that Hugh had been spreading, and knew whatever the issue was, it had never been resolved.

"Roy!" he yelled toward the blacksmith, and motioned for him to hurry. That was when Clay knocked Hugh to the ground. Ray started running and uttered a curse as Hugh's brother-in-law, Jose, came through the door carrying a shotgun. Ray pulled his own weapon and stopped at the edge of the sidewalk as Teresa jammed the barrel of her pistol against Jose's neck, daring him to shoot.

"Whoa, easy now. Everyone just calm down," he said as bystanders darted for cover. He gently took Teresa's wrist and moved the gun away from Jose's neck. "I'll take it from here."

The crowd came from out of hiding and gathered as Roy clambered up onto the sidewalk carrying his sledgehammer. "What's going on, Ray?"

"That's what I'm about to find out." He reached around Jose and grabbed the shotgun. "I'll take that too, if you don't mind. No, you just stand right there," he added as Jose started to leave. Hugh rolled to his belly with a loud moan and spit blood from his crushed lips.

"Okay, all of you, we're all going over to the jail and sort things out. I'm including you, Teresa," he added as she began collecting things that had spilled when she dropped the basket. Ray pointed toward a couple of bystanders. "Y'all give Hugh a hand. I don't think he knows which end is up."

"Never did," one of the men laughed as they helped him to his feet.

"Hell, Hugh," another snickered, "I thought you was supposed to be tough. At least, that's what you've been telling everyone. The way that feller beat the hell out of you, I think my daughter could whip you."

~ ~ ~

"Okay, let me hear your side of the story first, Clay. What got you riled enough to beat the stuffing outa Hugh?" Ray leaned back in his chair and rolled a cigarette.

"We was minding our own business, when this bag of guts comes out the door and starts making unkind remarks about Mrs. Romero's character. Being a Texan, I naturally took exception to the things he was saying, and thought I'd learn him some manners."

"That might be hard to do. What about you, Teresa? What'd Hugh say that got Clay pumped up?" Ray waited patiently while Teresa clamped her jaw tight and stared at the floor.

"I need a doctor," Hugh moaned. "I think this bastard busted my knee."

"You'll get a doctor when I say you can. Now, shut up." He turned back to Teresa.

"Well, he must've said something. What'd he say that started this whole thing?" He heaved a sigh as she kept quiet. "Damn, woman. You've got a tongue, don't ya? I'm not letting none of you go until I hear some answers. I'll lock y'all inside a cell if I have to…the whole bunch, including you."

"Is this the same fellow you've been telling me about?" Clay asked and pointed toward Hugh.

"*Si,*" she said quietly and nodded.

"Dammit!" Clay hissed. "I should've killed you when I had the chance," he said to Hugh.

"I'm starting to lose my patience with the whole lot of you," Ray said. "Is one of you gonna let me in on your secret?"

"From what I gather, a little over a year ago, Mrs. Romero invited this man over for supper, hoping to make friends. She figured maybe he'd like her cooking and hire her to cook for the cantina. It's tough on widows to make ends meet. Anyway, he took advantage of her and forced himself on her. Then he went around spreading rumors that she has loose morals. I really should've killed him," Clay said, rubbing his bruised knuckles. Ray looked at Teresa and shook his head.

"Is that true?"

She stared at the floor as a single tear trickled down her cheek.

"Did that really happen to you? Answer me!"

She nodded.

"That man raped you, and you never told me? Why didn't you say something?"

"What difference would it make?" she yelled. "I am a Mexican and he is white. Who would believe me? Would you?"

"Dammit woman!" Ray yelled, "you've got no call to say that to me. I've always treated Mexicans fair, and you know it. Maria is Mexican. Hugh certainly wouldn't have been walking around free and saying those things if you'd told me, that's for sure." He turned toward Hugh and raised his voice even louder.

"Great God Almighty, Hugh. I knew you were a bucket of pig guts, but I never thought you'd rape a woman...especially when you've got several whores working inside your cantina. What the hell's the matter with you?"

"Aw, Christ, Ray," Hugh said in disgust, "she asked for it. Inviting me over to her place and cooking a nice dinner and looking the way she does. Any man would think like I did. What would you think?"

"I'll tell you what I'd think, Hugh. I've eaten at her house and enjoyed a nice supper…even before Maria and me got married. And not once did I ever think about raping her. That's what I think."

"Well, maybe it's 'cause you're married to a Mexican."

"And so are you."

"Well…" Hugh dabbed at his lips with a hanky, "she ain't no innocent. Hell, she's got him living at her place," he pointed toward Clay, "and sleeping in her bed right now."

"That just shows how ignorant you are," Clay said with a snort. "I ain't sleeping in her bed like you think, and we certainly ain't lovers. I got tired of my personals getting rifled through at the hotel, and this woman was nice enough to rent me a cot at her place. Besides, she needed the money more than the hotel does, and the food's a hell of a lot better."

"Well, even if that's true…which it ain't, who cares? She's Mexican and I'm white. Who's gonna believe her over me?"

"*Carumba*, you are the son of many whores, and have a pig's heart," Jose said as he crossed the room. He bent over to get in Hugh's face. "You married my sister, and we both are Mexicans. I hope they hang you."

"Sit down Jose, I'll handle this. I don't know if they'll actually hang you, Hugh," Ray said as he lit his cigarette. "But to answer your question, I do. I believe her, that's who. And I also care. And I'm sure the jury will care, once they hear Mrs. Romero's story, and so will the circuit judge. And you'll start caring once you're busting rocks and building things for the great State of Texas."

~ ~   ~

They watched as Ray locked an angry Hugh Tullis inside a tiny cell next to the would-be bandits. "Do yourself a favor Ray," Clay said, clasping him on the shoulder. "Instead of waiting for just any judge, send a wire to San Antonio and request Judge Buford Stanley or his pa to hear this case. They're both good men, and they know Mrs. Romero personally. They'd love to try this one."

Clay took Teresa's arm and escorted her home. He sat in a chair smoking his pipe and watching Teresa as she fidgeted around the *jacale*. She tinkered with her pots and pans, and straightened bedding that had been made hours earlier. She unloaded her shopping basket, placing the items on the table and returned to her pots and pans without choosing one. Clay laid the pipe aside and took her by the shoulders.

"Hey," he said softly. "It's over. Everyone will know what really happened, and he won't bother you again. Ray and I will see to it."

She threw her arms around his neck and burst into tears. "Thank you… *Señor* Clay. You are a kind man. No one ever fights for me before." She kissed his cheek repeatedly. "Thank you, *señor*. Thank you."

He caressed the back of her head as her body heaved with each sob, wondering why no one had ever taken the time to listen. He believed there would never be another woman in his life besides June, but he could think of a million reasons for wanting to protect Teresa Romero.

Chapter 44

Jose hated to tell Marcela what her husband had done, and why he was locked in jail. He hated even more holding his only sister in his arms and feeling her hot tears against his shoulder. He had been against her marrying Hugh Tullis from the beginning. The big man was dirty and vulgar, and had a reputation for disliking Mexicans, as well as treating all women like whores. But Hugh had a lot of money, and owned the largest cantina in Carrizo Springs, so his sister refused to listen. She had been paying the price for her stubbornness for the past five years.

Jose had agreed to work at the cantina simply because he refused to leave his only sister unprotected in the clutches of such a beast. The man's insults toward Jose and Marcela had grown worse with each year, and the beatings he gave Marcela had increased in intensity as well as frequency. Jose hated himself for not doing something to stop the violence, but he was only half the size of Hugh, and had suffered a severe beating himself the only time he had tried. He thought about taking his sister and the children away in the middle of the night while Hugh was laid up with one of his whores. But traveling with a woman and small children in a wagon would be slow, and he was afraid what might happen if the man overtook them before they reached the safety of relatives in Mexico. The beating Hugh had received at the hands of Clay Best, and his arrest for the assault on Teresa Romero, had finally given him the chance he had been waiting for. His only concern was that Sheriff King could be right, and they may not hang Hugh for his crimes. That would leave the chance that Hugh might come looking for them once he was released.

Jose placed "closed" signs in the windows of the cantina and locked the doors, then emptied the cashbox and took all the valuables he could safely carry. He bought a wagon and two strong mules at Miguel's stable and packed their belongings. He told Marcela to prepare enough food for their trip to Fuente, Mexico where their brothers, Raul and Julio lived. They would find help and safety there. After the wagon had been loaded, he headed back to the stables.

"I hate to ask, but I need a big favor from you *amigo*," he said to Miguel.

"*Bien.* We have been friends for a long time. Go ahead and ask."

"I need you to take Marcela and her children in the wagon to Fuente while I take care of a few things. I will join you when I finish, and you will be free to return home."

"*Si,*" Miguel nodded, "I can go, but what will you be doing? Maybe we should wait until you have finished, then we will all go."

"No, you must go first, and don't ask what I'll be doing, *amigo.* It is best you don't know. I will join you on the road tomorrow night or the next morning, before you cross the river. If I don't come, that means something has happened, and I will not be coming. If that is the case, take her to our brothers in Fuente. She will know where they live."

Miguel nodded thoughtfully. "Are you sure about this, *amigo*? The last thing Marcela needs is for something to happen to you. What are you planning to do?"

"As I said, you don't need to know. Now will you help me?"

"*Si,*" Miguel nodded, "there is no need to ask."

~ ~   ~

179

Jose drove the wagon to the stable at dawn the next morning, where he kissed his sister and nephews goodbye. He then waited until they had completely disappeared before walking slowly back to the house where he took a nap. He woke several hours later and strolled around town, killing time and visiting with friends. He ate in one of the small cafes and took another nap. He waited until it had grown dark before saddling his horse and packing a few belongings into a saddle bag. He then entered the cantina from the rear entrance. The place was dark and smelled of rotting food from a fly-crusted pan of eggs and ham left on the stove. Jose poured himself two shots of tequila and downed them. He then waited an hour longer before leaving out the back and climbing onto this horse. Miguel must certainly be nearing Eagle Pass by now. He walked his horse silently up to the rear of the jail and leaned close to one of the barred windows.

"Pssst! *Señor* Hugh. Are you awake? I have come for you."

Hugh Tullis had been lying on the cot, concocting a plan of revenge on Clay Best and Teresa Romero. He sat upright at the sound of Jose's voice.

"Huh?"

"I said I have come for you. Here, at the window."

Hugh stood on the edge of the cot and leaned his face against the bars.

"Over here. The next window," he said in a loud whisper. Hugh was expecting Jose to slip him a gun, or perhaps a bottle of tequila. He gasped as his brother-in-law jammed a pistol against his forehead, then pulled the trigger.

Jose turned his horse and galloped toward the west edge of town and toward the Mexican border before the single deputy on night-duty could summon Sheriff King. Jose smiled, knowing Hugh Tullis would never mistreat his sister or any other woman again...ever.

Chapter 45

Teresa flew out of bed and wrapped a robe around her body at the sound of pounding on her door. Clay jumped to his feet and lit the lamp.

"Wait a second," he yelled as the pounding grew louder. He grabbed Teresa's arm as she started toward the door. "Hold on a minute." He quickly tossed back the blankets on Teresa's bed and rumpled the pillow. "Makes things look right," he said as Teresa gave him a questioning look. What he had told Ray King was only a half-truth. It was true they had never had sex, but they had been sleeping in the same bed when the pounding woke them. Teresa nodded and opened the door.

"*Señor* Ray," Teresa pulled the robe tightly and stepped back, "please come in. What is it?"

"It's Hugh Tullis. Someone put a bullet through his head. Y'all wouldn't know anything about that, would you?"

"Hell, Ray, you know me better'n that," Clay said. He laid the pistol he had been holding on the table and packed tobacco into his pipe. "If I'd really wanted to kill that polecat, I'd have done it at the cantina in front of God and everyone."

"That's what I figured, but I still had to ask. After all, you did say a couple of times inside my office that you wished you had killed him."

"I might've said it, but he didn't need killing. He needed to be taught a lesson. I kind of figured like you, bustin' rocks and clearing trails in the hot sun for a year or two would've been better than killing him outright." Clay lit the pipe and drew deeply. "Got any idee who might've done it?"

"I figure it was more'n likely Jose. I've been all over at their place and Marcela and the kids are gone. Jose also vanished along with all the money inside the cantina's cashbox. It ain't no secret how Jose felt about his sister and how he hated her husband. They're more'n likely halfway to Mexico by now."

"Want me to go with you and track him down?"

"Na," Ray shook his head slowly, "they'll make the border by the time we catch up with them. Besides, I figure Carrizo Springs might be better off without Hugh Tullis." He glanced at both beds and nodded. "Sorry to disturb your sleep." Ray touched the brim of his hat and disappeared into the dark.

Teresa slowly closed the door and turned to stare at Clay. He wrapped her in his arms and kissed the top of her head.

"See, I told you it was over. He'll never bother you, or say another bad word about anyone. Someone's done sent him to hell where he belongs."

Chapter 46

They sat on horseback, staring at the empty street as several tumbleweeds chased a cloud of dust through the middle of town. The stables that had once been filled with horses and mules now stood empty. The door to Raul and Maria's house banged loudly, keeping rhythm with the gusting wind. Clay dismounted and walked slowly past the stone fire pit where Maria had once baked tortillas and sung songs. He latched the door and gazed sadly at the empty corral. There were no laughing children playing with their dog and pet goat. The bank as well as the general store had "closed" signs hanging in their windows. There were no women gossiping on the sidewalks, or dogs barking happily after children as they chased each other down the street. The only building that had the appearance of being open was the saloon.

"*Carumba, Señor* Clay, what happened? Where is everyone?" Teresa slid gracefully to the ground.

"I don't rightly know, but I aim to find out." Clay took the reins from her gloved hand and led the horses toward the saloon. Teresa swatted dust from her skirt as he tied the reins to the hitching post. The place looked empty and smelled of dust and stale whiskey when they entered. It took several seconds for Clay's eyes to adjust before he spied Lester Bishop slumped over a bottle at his favorite table in the far corner. Clay ran his fingers across the nearest table, leaving lines in about a week's worth of dust. Charlie came from the store room carrying a case of whiskey and stacked it on a handcart with several others.

"Well, howdy Clay. Ma'am," he said and gave Teresa nod. "I never figured I'd see y'all back here. Did you ever find out what happened to Ruth?"

"Ruth's doing just fine, Charlie. She got shed of that polecat she run off with, and married herself a prominent circuit judge."

"Ya don't say?" Charlie laughed.

"Yes sir, and they're expecting to have themselves a baby."

"Well, I'll be a suck-egg mule. I sure hope she ain't planning on moving back here."

"Not a chance." Clay glanced around the room. "What the hell happened while we was gone, Charlie? I knew the town was dying, but it looks as though someone put it out of its misery."

"Someone did." Charlie poured three brandies and toasted them before downing his. "Those two slingers Lester hired finally figured Les' word wasn't worth spit, and up and quit on him. The only thing is, they robbed the bank and killed ol' Chester in the process. I guess the dumb bastard figured the money inside that vault belonged to him instead of Lester, and he put up an argument. I don't know which one, but either Curley or Westfall put two .45 slugs in his gizzard. Then they took it all…every last cent." He refilled their glasses and snickered as he shook his head.

"Raul and Maria pulled out three days ago."

"Got any idee where they were heading?"

"Mexico. Raul's folks own a farm somewhere south of the Rio Bravo. I don't know where exactly. I asked them to leave me a rig and a team of mules. It's parked out back right now. They took everything else, and I can't say as I blame 'em. Les hadn't been paying them for the past few months either.

"I'm the last living soul left, outside of Les, and I've been hanging around just to see what he's gonna do…and you see it. Right over there." He toasted the drunk at the corner table and downed his brandy. "I reminded him several times he owes me two month's back wages, and he keeps saying he'll get it out of the bank in San Antonio. But the truth is, he ain't got anything in any bank to pay me with…not a copper to his name."

"Got any idee where them two scallywags took off to?" Clay asked. His eyes followed Teresa as she crossed the room and stood with her hands on her hips staring at Lester's balding head lying against the table.

"No, I wish I did. I had most of my money inside that bank, and they took it. I kind of figured I'd do like Raul and take my wages in stock from the back room. Most of the stuff is rotgut, but Les did have some pretty good private stock he kept mostly for hisself. I'm taking that too. I figure to leave him enough rotgut to finish himself off, and find someplace where I can open my own saloon."

"Huh," Clay chuckled and downed his brandy, "this might be your lucky day, Charlie. The owner of the cantina in Carrizo Springs got hisself killed last night. I figure they might welcome a new owner about now. Thanks for the brandy."

"No problem, Clay. I'll stop in Carrizo Springs and see if that's a possibility. Anytime you and the lady want a drink, it's on me."

Clay crossed the room to stand beside Teresa. She shook her head in disgust.

"Hey, *hombre*," she said in a loud voice. Lester gave no sign of hearing her. She heaved a sigh as she grabbed a handful of gray hair and jerked him upright in the chair.

"*Hombre*, it is not nice to ignore someone when they speak to you. *Señor* Clay has found your granddaughter for you. Now he wishes for you to pay him one thousand American dollars. Understand me, *hombre*?"

Lester stared at her through bloodshot eyes and snickered. His face was puffy and red, and he wobbled as he leaned back in his chair.

"Yeah? You found Ruth? Where is she?"

"She's with her husband," Clay said. "She got married to a Judge Stanley up in San Antonio, and they're fixin' to have a young-un. You ought to be right proud of her. Now, Mrs. Romero and me would like to get paid, if you have anything left."

"Na-uh," Lester shook his head as he poured himself another drink, "the deal was for you to find her *and* bring her home. I don't see any Ruth, so you ain't gonna see any money."

"No sir, I agreed to find her, but I never agreed to bring her back to this hellhole," Clay said. "Besides, she doesn't want to come, and I don't think Judge Stanley would take it too kindly if I tried forcing her to. Here's a picture of the happy couple, if you're interested." Clay tossed a copy of the San Antonio Examiner on the table and Lester immediately swept it to the floor.

"Get the hell out of here and bring Ruth back like I told you to, you son-of-a-bitch!"

Teresa whipped one of the pearl-handled pistols from her holster and Clay jerked her arm upward as she fired. Particles of dust fell from the ceiling and landed on the table as the glass slipped from Lester's hand and hit the table, spilling its contents across a half-played deck of cards.

"Easy, easy," Clay said, taking the gun from her hand as she struggled.

"But… *Señor* Clay, this…pig is cheating us!"

"Sure he is. But killing him would only put him out of his misery. Take a good look at him." Clay gestured toward Lester. "He's a busted-down old drunk, who's set on drinking hisself to death. He ain't shaved or taken a bath in a week of Sundays. The shirt looks like it's been wallowed on by a pig, and he smells like a sivet-cat. He probably ain't got more'n a month or two before he rots away on the inside and dies. Once we leave, there won't even be anyone to bury him. He'll just sit there and rot, unless some coyote wanders in here and carts him off. So just let 'em be. Killing will only make it easier on him."

"You and your Mexican whore can get the hell out of my saloon," Lester yelled as he pointed a shaking finger toward the door.

"Oh, we're leaving alright, and I doubt that I'll ever be back this way again, unless it's to see your rotting bones. See, the thing is, I know them two slingers stole what money you had, and you ain't got enough to pay for your own drinks, let alone pay us for finding Ruth. Besides, Ruth don't want any part of you. The fact is, nobody else does either. You're all alone Les. Even the whores left." Clay snickered as he scooped the joker from the table and tossed it in front of Lester. 'You played the joker once too often, Les, and lost everything."

Clay took Teresa by the arm and ignored Lester's curses as he turned away. They could hear Charlie's voice as they left the saloon.

"See, I told you, you old miserable son-of-a-bitch. You're getting exactly what you deserve. I'll be gone in another hour, so you'll have to get your own bottle from now on."

"Where the hell do you think you're going? I didn't say you could leave."

"You've go no say in the matter. And don't try stopping me, 'cause I'll kill you, Les. You know I will…you rotten bastard."

Chapter 47

"What is wrong, *Señor* Clay?" Teresa had been kneeling beside June's grave, praying, when she looked up to see the expression on Clay's face.

"Wrong? Nothing's wrong," Clay said shaking his head. "It's just that she ain't here no more."

"*¿Qué?* Is this not *Señora* Best's grave?"

"Sure, it's where June was buried alright, but she ain't here anymore. It's like her spirit's left. I used to be able to stand here and feel her presence, but it ain't here anymore. It's like she finally figured I'm gonna be alright and went on to heaven."

"She does." Teresa held her hand for Clay to take as she stood.

"She does what?"

"The *señora* knows you will be alright. I promised her in my prayers I will take care of you."

Clay stared at her as they walked slowly toward his old house.

"Ya did, huh? You promised June you'd take care of me?"

"*Sí.*" She nodded.

"Now, why would you do something like that?"

"Because I love you, and I want to take care of you."

"Oh." They reached the front porch to find Antonio asleep in the shade where they had left him.

"So, what do we do now, *Señor* Clay?" Teresa said after a long silence.

"I've got no idea what I'm gonna do. I guess you're free to do whatever you want."

"*Si*, but I already tell you, I do whatever you are doing, because I promised to take care of you."

Clay took her by the shoulders and searched her face.

"Now, why in God's name would a young, beautiful woman like you want to tag along beside an old busted-down lawman like me? You could have most any man you choose."

"*Señor*, you are stubborn and have a head like Miguel's goat." She tapped the side of his head with her fingers. "I tell you every day how my heart feels," she patted her breast, "and say I love you, yet you still don't understand? I will never leave you, *señor*, and you cannot leave without me. Now, I ask you one more time, what are we going to do now?"

"Well, since you put it that way, I don't rightly know." Clay shoved both hands in his pockets and leaned against the wall. "I spent most of the money I had finding Ruth. Beyond that, I ain't got anything to offer you except this house in the middle of a town with no people. I reckon I'll just have to find some way of making a living. The thing is, I don't know anything but cowboying and being a lawman. Maybe someone's hiring in Carrizo Springs."

Teresa pursed her lips thoughtfully and nodded. "That is *no importante*. We have our *casa* in Carrizo Springs to live in. If it is the money that worries you *señor*, there is no need to worry, I have money."

"Huh?" Clay cocked his head and creased his eyebrows.

"I say I have money…a lot of money I think. But we have to go to Mexico to get it."

"If you've got money, why didn't you say something before now? The bigger question is, why don't you go get it and open your restaurant like you've been saying?"

"Because it will be dangerous. Before the Comanches kill Refugio, he is in charge of a regiment of General Bernal's revolutionaries. They robbed a Federale train that is carrying...*cómo se dice*..." she tried grabbing the words with her fingers.

"Payroll?"

"*Si*," she nodded, "and it has much gold. Refugio and his men take all the gold. My Refugio, he hided the gold in a cave by a waterfall near an old hacienda in Mexico. He tells me where it is in case something happens, so I can tell General Bernal. But General Bernal never comes to Carrizo Springs so I can tell him where the gold is hided." Teresa shrugged her shoulders. "I never know why he doesn't come."

"And you think the gold is still there?"

Teresa nodded.

"What's stopping the rest of the men who rode with your husband from getting it?"

"There were three revolutionaries with Refugio when they hided the gold, and those three died when the Comanches killed Refugio. So they cannot get the gold, *Señor* Clay. I think the gold is still there."

"How much gold are we talking about?"

Teresa shrugged her shoulders. "It takes a wagon to carry the gold, and it will be dangerous. There are the Federales who wish to have the gold back. Then there is the Comanche and Mescalero Apache. There is also the Yaqui who do not like Mexicans or Americanos. We will have to be very careful."

Clay turned away thoughtfully as he packed fresh tobacco into his pipe, then took his time lighting it.

"Do you know where this place is?"

"*Si*, I was born in the hacienda. It belonged to my mother and father, and they were there when the Comanche killed them. My mother's little sister was with us when they come. She was very young, and I was only *dos, quizá tres años*, old." She held up two, then three fingers. "My aunt was playing with me by the waterfall when the Comanches come, and she hided with me inside the cave. The Comanche do not see us, but my mother and father are working in the bean field, and they die. They burned the hacienda and my aunt's father sees the smoke and comes to help, but it is too late. The Comanches are gone. He takes me to my grandmother in Carrizo Springs and tells her what happened and she tells me when I am older. I visit my uncle once, and he showed where I was born, and where my mama and papa are buried. Nobody goes there now because it is dangerous. My uncle is afraid and moves his family to Mexico City. Indians water their horses in the creek, but they never go into the cave because it makes noise in the wind. They say it has a bad spirit, that's why it is hided behind the waterfall. I showed Refugio where my aunt hided me, and that is where he hided the gold. I think it is still there, *Señor* Clay."

Clay puffed silently on the pipe until Teresa began to wonder if he believed her story. "It would be best to take a couple of mules and pack out what we can carry and leave the rest for later," he said absently.

"Then we go, *Señor* Clay?"

"Yes, Mrs. Romero, we go. But we need to go back to Carrizo Springs first, to get a couple of mules and pack in some supplies. Then," he took her by the shoulders and gave her a quick kiss on the lips, "we need to see the priest."

"*¿Qué?* Why do we need to see a priest to get my gold?"

"Because I'm sick and tired of trying to sleep with you all cuddled-up next to me when I can't touch you. I never cheated on June when she was alive, and I certainly ain't gonna do it while she's dead. If we're gonna take care of each other, we're gonna make it legal. In short, Mrs. Romero, we're changing your name from Romero to Best. Understand?"

"*Si, muy bien.* That is good for me."

She grabbed Clay in a tight hug and kissed him. She was still clinging to him when a single wagon filled with whiskey and several barrels of cheap beer rolled past. The driver smiled and waved as he turned the team of mules toward Carrizo Springs.

END

About The Authors

MAJOR MITCHELL (pictured on the left), is the author of four historical westerns and two children's books. He lives with his wife, Judy, in Northern California. A member of The Western Writers of America and a frequent guest speaker at historical meetings and schools on the west coast, he has also written several songs, and takes the stage on rare occasions as a singer.

JERRY MITCHELL (pictured on the right), is the author of several short stories and lives with this wife, Juana, in Northern California, approximately 45 minutes from his brother Major. His ideas have been the inspiration for two of Major's novels.

More about the authors, their books and photo gallery may be found at www.majormitchell.net.

Correspondence for both authors should be addressed to:

Shalako Press
P.O. Box 371
Oakdale, CA 95361-0371

http://www.shalakopress.com

*For your reading pleasure, we invite you to
visit our Trading Post bookstore.*

Canyon Wind
The Doña
Mokelumne Gold
Poverty Flat
Dusty Boots
Manhunter
Where A Good Wind Blows
The Horseman And The Cowgirls
A Reason To Believe
Charlie Shepherd (children's)
The Witch On Oak Street (children's)

Shalako Press

http://www.shalakopress.com